THE ENDSISTER

Penni Russon

D1350881

ALLEN&UNWIN

SYDNEY · MELBOURNE · AUCKLAND · LONDON

First published by Allen & Unwin in 2018

A version of *The Endsister* was first serialised on Storybird.com

Copyright © Penni Russon, 2018

All rights reserved. No part of this book may be reproduced or transmitted in any
form or by any means, electronic or mechanical, including photocopying, recording
or by any information storage and retrieval system, without prior permission in
writing from the publisher. The Australian *Copyright Act 1968* (the Act) allows a
maximum of one chapter or ten per cent of this book, whichever is the greater,
to be photocopied by any educational institution for its educational purposes
provided that the educational institution (or body that administers it) has given
a remuneration notice to the Copyright Agency (Australia) under the Act.

Allen & Unwin
83 Alexander Street
Crows Nest NSW 2065
Australia
Phone: (61 2) 8425 0100
Email: info@allenandunwin.com
Web: www.allenandunwin.com

A Cataloguing-in-Publication entry is available
from the National Library of Australia
www.trove.nla.gov.au

ISBN 9 78 174175 065 2

For teaching resources, explore www.allenandunwin.com/resources/for-teachers

Cover and text design by Sandra Nobes
Cover illustration by Sandra Eterović
Set in 11/15.5 pt Minion Pro by Midland Typesetters, Australia
Colour reproduction by Splitting Image, Clayton, Victoria

Printed in Australia by McPherson's Printing Group

10 9 8 7 6 5 4 3 2 1

www.pennirusson.com

The paper in this book is FSC® certified.
FSC® promotes environmentally responsible,
socially beneficial and economically viable
management of the world's forests.

THE ENDSISTER

Other books by Penni Russon

Only Ever Always
Dear Swoosie (with Kate Constable)
Little Bird
Indigo Girls

The Undine Trilogy
Undine
Breathe
Drift

FOR AVERY

IN THE LOCKED attic of the house on Mortlake Road in south-west London, near a bend in the River Thames, something stirs.

It shudders, a cobwebbed thing, tattered and dusty, so long forgotten, so long forgetting.

It is hardly anything, but it is almost something, disturbing the shadows, shrinking from the approaching light.

SIBBI

SHADOWS OF GUM trees grow long across the paddocks.
Light is low and syrupy. The light of time shifting: day into
evening, summer into autumn.

Here comes Sibbi Outhwaite, four years old, wild as the
shadows and the sun, belonging as much to the hills and
the valley as the wind in the pale whispery grass. Down
she comes. Down the kangaroo track, a rocky narrow path
that leads from the wooden house on the rise to Aunty May
Wilson's house by the road that sweeps through the valley.
Sibbi clutches a bouquet of wilting wildflowers in her fist.

Aunty May's house squats low and silent. Sibbi knocks on
the back door and tries the handle. It is locked. She stumps
around the veranda, her gumboots thudding on the wooden
boards, and knocks on the front door. She calls through the
laundry window, always left open.

'Cooee? Cooee, Aunty May?' Then: 'Kitty! Kitty-kitty!'
But not even the old brown cat comes out to rub against her
leg or push his insistent head up under her hand.

Sibbi lays the wildflowers she's picked carefully on the front doorstep and plays, laying out pieces of broken sticks in the dust – Mama Stick, Papa Stick, Sister Stick, Brother Stick and Aunty Stick. Aunty May's yard and the fields and bushland all around are all an extension of Sibbi's backyard. This is one big property – the wooden house on the hill that Sibbi's family rents belongs to Aunty May. Aunty May was born in the hill house, just like Sibbi.

The emptiness of the valley house unsettles Sibbi now. She feels a creeping sensation at the back of her neck, as if the crouching house, or something in the house, is watching her. She turns to go back up the kangaroo track. She hears the cat's lonely *marraow* inside the house. The sound frightens her and she runs up the hill towards home.

Sibbi's mama, Olly, is in the yard unpegging clothes from the washing line.

'Aunty May wasn't home,' says Sibbi.

'That's odd. Are you sure?'

'I knocked. Loud louder loudest. But nobody came.'

'That's very odd. Maybe her nephew came to take her out?'

It's funny to Sibbi that everyone calls Aunty May 'Aunty' except her nephew and his wife, who call her just May.

'Missus Wilson to youse,' the nephew's wife once told the Outhwaite kids. But Aunty May is Aunty May, same as Daddy is Daddy, Mama is Mama and Else, Clancy and the twins are Else, Clancy and the twins. Same as the moon is the moon, same as apples is apples.

Sibbi forgets about Aunty May until her daddy comes home in the rattling van. Daddy has stopped at the post office to pick up the mail, but he throws the unopened pile of envelopes bound together with a rubber band on the bench. He has a frowning worried face and news of Aunty May.

ELSE

'Mei-Ling in the post office told me Aunty May was taken to hospital in an ambulance last night,' Dave tells us.

'I saw the ambulance,' I say, helping myself to a slice of lasagne.

There is a meat one for the twins, Dave and Sibbi; veggie for Olly, Clancy and me.

'You did not,' say Oscar.

'I saw the lights, but then I went back to sleep and when I woke up I thought it must have been a dream. I didn't even remember until now.'

Not proper remembering, anyway, though the blue light did flash into my mind once or twice during the day, the way a really strong dream revisits you long after you've woken up. Of course, I never thought anything was wrong with Aunty May. It was just the light I thought of, blue and ghostly, sliding around the walls, intermittently lighting up Sibbi's face on the other side of our small, shared room.

'She's getting on a bit,' says Dave.

'She's only eighty,' says Olly. 'And she's been so fit and active.'

'Is it serious?' Clancy asks. 'Is she going to –'

'It's a bit of a worry.' And that's all Dave will say.

CLANCY

AFTER DINNER, MUM and Dad stay together in the kitchen to wash up, which is usually the children's job. Us kids go out onto the veranda. The twins spread their footy swap cards out, but hardly look at them.

I hold a breathing knitted bundle – Hester the ringtail possum, wrapped in an old woollen jumper of Mum's. I found Hester in her mother's pouch, after the mum got caught in a wire fence on a neighbouring property. Later Hester'll scuttle up the wooden beam of the veranda and onto the roof and then into the gum tree whose branches swing over the house. She spends every night out of doors, active as any possum, but she still likes to spend days sleeping in the jumper, even though she's almost old enough to look after herself.

I see Aunty May's nephew's car beetle along the road to Aunt May's house. We all look down from the veranda as the nephew gets out and goes into the house.

'It's not just Aunty May they're worried about,' Else says.

'It's our house. Her nephew will want to sell it. We'll have to move.'

'He can't sell it,' says Finn. 'We live here.'

'When Aunty May dies, it will belong to him. We're just renting from Aunty May.'

'What's renting?' Oscar asks.

'Where you pay someone money every week to live in their house. Aunty May doesn't charge us very much, either. Mum and Dad will be worrying about money.'

'Don't we have money?' asks Sibbi.

I guess Sibbi doesn't know much about money yet. She knows there is money in Mum's purse, in Dad's pocket, and in the bank. Sometimes there is money on the floor of the van, and sometimes there is money in the crack behind the cushions of the couch. But sometimes we all scrounge and search, and there's no money in the cushions or under the van's seats or anywhere.

'We're not rich,' says Else, who knows more about it than even me. 'We've got enough to get by, but not much more. If we had to pay more rent, that would be a struggle.'

'I wish we could afford to buy Aunty May's house from the nephew,' says Finn.

We watch the nephew come out of Aunty May's house with what looks like a plastic shopping bag full of clothes hooked on his arm and the brown cat wedged firmly under his armpit. With some difficulty he gets both into the hatchback of his car. Briefly, he looks up at us, shielding his eyes against the sun not quite set behind our house. When he sees us, he raises one arm. Sibbi waves back. We watch him drive away.

CLANCY

I LIKE THE time I spend in the morning with Mum. We sit together in companionable silence, in the brief lull before the twins are shaken awake and Sibbi is roused and, last of all, Else emerges, somehow completely ready to go, make-up on, hair brushed, furious with everyone else for holding her up.

The mail Dad collected from the post office yesterday still sits on the kitchen bench. One envelope catches my eye. It's narrower than the ordinary envelopes with their typewritten addresses behind plastic windows. It's a creamy colour, addressed by hand, like an invitation or something.

'What's this?' I hand it to Mum, noticing the Queen on the stamp in the corner.

Mum opens the envelope with a butter knife.

'Dave!' she calls. Dad comes into the kitchen rubbing his hair with a towel. I can see a bit of shaving foam bubbling near his ear.

'Read this.'

He scans it. Sits down and reads it again.

'Is it real?' says Mum.

'It looks real.'

'But how can we –?' says Mum, just as Dad says, 'It makes sense, who else would there be?'

I'm used to hearing my parents talking like this, in half sentences, like some kind of code. It's a small house and there's so many of us, they don't get much of a chance to talk without one of us listening. Of all of us, I am the best at disappearing into the woodwork, not jumping to conclusions, not flapping about squawking like Oscar or Else. Usually if I stay quiet and don't interrupt, Mum and Dad forget I'm here. But today they're giving nothing away.

'How could we?' says Mum. 'What will the children say?'

'We can't tell them,' says Dad. 'Not yet.'

'Tell us what?' I ask, finally.

'Nothing,' says Mum.

'It would be *something* though, wouldn't it?' says Dad, his eyes bright, staring intensely at Mum. 'It would be really something. The next chapter.'

'Yes,' Mum agrees, though she sounds less sure. 'It would certainly be something.'

ELSE

I LAY MY violin across my lap and reattach my shoulder rest. My limbs feel heavy and stupid. It's an effort to lift the instrument back up under my chin.

I place the bow on the A string, knowing what's coming next.

'Right,' says Adrian. 'Now you've warmed up, let's try the Mozart.'

I begin, holding my breath. I feel Adrian bristling as I labour my way through the first bars.

'No,' says Adrian. 'Like this.' And his bow leaps across the notes.

He has me play the first sixteen bars again and again, until finally he snaps, 'Enough! Take a break.'

'I just can't get it,' I say, hearing a whine in my voice. 'It just doesn't make sense to me. Why can't I play something easier?'

'This is the perfect piece for you,' Adrian insists. 'It's right in the sweet spot of your ability, with enough challenge to make you work. And you can play it, you know the notes. But there's no musicality. There's nothing of you in it.'

I scowl.

'Listen,' he says. 'You're good and you know it. You could almost be brilliant. But do you know how many almost brilliant sixteen-year-old violinists there are in Australia? Plenty. More than enough to fill every seat in every orchestra, quartet, chamber group, ensemble and alt gypsy folk rock band in every city, town, and backwater across the country. It takes more than talent to be a professional.'

'Maybe I don't want to be professional,' I say. Something inside me, some new wound, splits open as I say it, but my voice comes out wooden, with no emotion at all.

'Well, it's an expensive hobby,' Adrian snaps back. 'If you're not serious, maybe you don't need a teacher anymore. You already know enough to play for fun.'

Fun? I can't remember the last time playing violin was fun! Adrian thinks I haven't been practising, that I'm lazy. But he's wrong. I've practised and practised the Mozart, working every morning and afternoon in my bedroom. I can't make it into anything more than a haphazard collection of notes. The harder I work the more broken it is, the more nonsensical it sounds.

At the end of my lesson, Adrian says, 'You know, Else. It's pretty normal for people your age to stop lessons, if they've taken the instrument as far as they can. There's no shame in it. Do you want me to talk to your parents for you?'

'No,' I say. 'I'll try harder.'

Adrian frowns. 'Well, let's not waste anyone's time. I don't want to keep teaching you if you're not going to practise.

I'd rather put my energy into students who are self-motivated.'
He turns to me and bows. I bow back.

'I'd say thank you for the lesson,' Adrian says, 'but I don't think either of us were feeling it today. We'll do better next time, okay?'

I nod. I say, 'Okay.'

SIBBI

SIBBI AND HER father spend an ordinary sort of day together cleaning the windows, sweeping out the kitchen, weeding the vegetable patch, reading stories, making a casserole for tea and dressing up as rather untidy princesses and running around under the pear trees frightening the birds. Daddy makes a magnificent princess because he is so tall.

They go together to Aunty May's lonesome cottage and feed the chooks and collect the eggs, then climb the hill back up to their own little house, Sibbi's hand squeezed tight inside Daddy's big hand. She doesn't like to see the little house look so alone-ly.

Daddy brings down a box of photographs. Some are very, very old, stiff and brittle brownish in colour. They show olden days people, dressed in very formal clothes with serious faces.

Daddy says, 'It took so long to take a photograph that it was a very serious business. Cameras were so slow in the old days that people had to stand still for a very long time.'

'Who's that?' Sibbi asks, pointing to a girl who, despite her old-fashioned clothes and hairstyle, reminds her of Else. It's in her stubborn, sulking chin, but also the sparkly eyes, as if this girl also knows mischief and silliness and fun.

'An ancestor,' Daddy says. He is shuffling through coloured photographs now, square prints with white borders. 'Look,' he says, showing Sibbi a photo of a smallish, roundish boy and a shadowy smiling lady with heavy rimmed glasses and a dress with a shirt collar sitting on a rumpled green lawn, squinting into the camera. The boy has gingery curly hair like Clancy's. Whoever is taking the photo has not done a very good job, because the boy and the lady are crowded into one corner, and the rest of the photo is garden and willow tree and sky.

'Is that an ancestor too?'

Daddy laughs. 'That's me! And my Aunt Dorothy. This was taken in Kensington Gardens, I think. In London, anyway.'

'Is London in the city?'

'London *is* a city. It's a city in a country called England, a very long way away from here, on the other side of the world.'

Sibbi's face lights up with recognition. 'It's where the pussycat went.'

'Is it?' Daddy asks, distracted, still looking at the photo.

Sibbi gets down from the table and goes to her room to get her book of nursery rhymes. She brings it back to the table and pushes it up in front of Daddy, then climbs up onto his knee. She helps him find the right page and he reads aloud, 'Pussycat, pussycat, where have you been? I've been to London to visit the Queen.'

'Is there really a queen there? In London?'

'Yes,' Daddy tells her. 'And a prince called William married to a princess called Kate.'

'Do they have any babies?'

'A boy called George and a girl called Charlotte, I think.'

'Can I go there and visit Baby Prince George and Baby Princess Charlotte?'

'I don't think they are really babies anymore. They're little kids like you.'

'I'm not a little kid. I'm a big girl.'

'Well, George and Charlotte are big too.'

'I'm a big girl baby. And Prince George is a big boy prince baby. We could visit the Queen.'

'Well,' says Daddy, leafing through the nursery rhyme book, 'she seems to be quite busy eating bread and honey and making tarts and being visited by pussycats.'

'Does it take a long time to get to London?'

'A night and a day,' says Daddy. 'On a big aeroplane called a jumbo jet.'

'Does it cost a lot of money?' Sibbi asks, remembering what Else said about being almost poor.

'An awful lot. Yes. Thousands and thousands of dollars for Mama and me and the twins and Else and Clancy and you. So we'd want to be sure, before we went.'

'Sure of what?'

Daddy gathers up the photographs. 'Well, that the Queen was going to be home, of course.'

'And Baby Prince George?'

'Oh yes. Definitely Baby Prince George. We wouldn't want to waste a trip.'

ALMOST ANNIE
AND HARDLY ALICE

ONE RAIN-STREAKED MORNING, almost a century ago now, Almost Annie woke up dead to find Hardly Alice looming over her. Almost Annie recalled her own life in startling detail, but Hardly Alice claimed to have no memory of who she was before her death.

Hardly Alice wore beautifully made clothes in fine fabrics, but they seemed old-fashioned to Almost Annie. Her corset was straight and unflattering, and her skirt had hoops and no bustle, so she must have lived and died many years before Annie had taken her position in Mortlake Road.

From the way she spoke, it was clear Hardly Alice had been well born, a daughter of the house. Almost Annie was a lowly nurserymaid; by today's standards, she was not much more than a child herself when she died. She was some years, but not many, younger than Hardly Alice, who looked on the verge of grown up.

'Oh, larks,' says Hardly Alice. 'Look who's just pulled up in that black cab. It's that dreary law-man, Old Whatshisname.'

'Mr Brompton, and it's not his fault he looks like that.'

'Well, it's not my fault, either,' says Hardly Alice. 'He has the countenance of a man who has lost his favourite cheese and a great deal more besides.'

'He is always very good to Our Dorothy.'

Hardly Alice sniffs. 'I dare say he has killed her off. He'll turn the house into some sort of inn and let out the rooms to Scotsmen.'

'Oh, wouldn't that be lovely?' says Almost Annie. 'Do you think they'll bring their children? Not,' she hastens to add, 'that I am wishing ill on poor Miss Dorothy.'

'Look out, here he comes.'

'Do you think Dorothy is coming home?' Annie asks.

Alice gives Annie a pitying look. 'No,' she says bluntly. 'I don't think Dorothy is coming home.'

The key rattles in the lock and the great heavy door crashes open. A flash of daylight and street noise enters the house and so does Mr Brompton, leading a pair of young men in work gear into the house.

'Oh, look! That one has got one of those hand-held computer devices.' Hardly Alice drifts up behind the young man's shoulder, watching with rapt interest as the man taps and sweeps his finger on the glass screen.

'Still in quite original condition, I see,' says one of the men.

'He means ghastly,' Hardly Alice says.

'There's nothing wrong with it,' says Almost Annie.

'It's been very well cared for,' says Brompton.

'It's an abomination,' says Hardly Alice. She and Almost Annie have watched enough episodes of *Grand Designs* with Dorothy Outhwaite to know how hopelessly dated the big house is.

The ghost girls wander around the house, looking at it through the men's eyes. The one with the iPad flicks up the dust sheets and makes notes about the furniture beneath.

'Some of these bits might be worth a few bob, I suppose,' the other young man says. 'You could sell it as a job lot to an auction house, I should think. We can sort that out for you. Unless you were planning to sell the house furnished?'

'Oh, it's not selling. It's to stay in the family. It's been inherited by a nephew in Australia.'

The two young men catch each other's eyes. 'Poor sod. It's a lot of work.'

'This house has good bones, anyone can see that,' says Annie to Alice. She is fond of Kevin from *Grand Designs*. He has a timeless sort of charm. But she does not fancy the modern houses, with their gleaming surfaces and empty spaces. She thinks Outhwaite House is just fine the way it is.

Hardly Alice sniffs. She'd like nothing better than to see the entire house gutted and reappointed with all the latest fittings. Gleaming, shining surfaces. Splashbacks and concrete floors. The industrial look.

The humans and ghosts leave the drawing room and wander through the kitchen and scullery and out into the garden, then back through the large reception room and up the stairs to the big room and Dorothy Outhwaite's study and then up another flight of stairs to three bedrooms

The cleaners make notes on all the rooms – two beds in the big room on the middle floor, bunk beds for one upstairs bedroom, a single bed for the second upstairs room, and a queen for the master bedroom – until there's just one door left.

'No!' cries Almost Annie and Hardly Alice hisses violently.

'I haven't a key to that room,' says Brompton, firmly. 'It's only a storage closet or something, I believe.'

The cleaner gives the handle a twist, rattling the door vigorously, but it remains stuck fast.

'But *why* don't we want them to go in there?' Almost Annie asks, but of course Hardly Alice, if she has ever known, does not remember.

In all the time Almost Annie has haunted this house and even before, when she was still alive and in service, this particular door has remained locked. As a ghost she can roam freely through the entire house, even into rooms forbidden to her as a nurserymaid, as far as the back garden wall, but this door is as impenetrable to her as the front door to Mortlake Road and the wider world.

She and Hardly Alice sit on the stairs and watch Brompton and the cleaners leave the house together. Everything settles back into a deep, still silence.

'Bored,' says Hardly Alice. 'I wish I had one of those screens to play with.'

'Devil's work,' says Annie.

But their squabble is interrupted before it begins, when Brompton comes back into the house. He stands in the hallway and clears his throat. He stares blindly at the landing above their heads. 'It is my unfortunate duty to tell you that Miss Dorothy Outhwaite has recently passed away.'

'Well, obviously,' Hardly Alice murmurs to Annie. 'Such a strange, pasty, little man.'

'Oh, do be quiet,' says Almost Annie. And she goes upstairs to find solitude. It turns out even ghosts can grieve the dead.

ELSE

I STAND AT the kitchen sink, looking down at the roof of Aunty May's house. Some last pale rays of sun are making their way through the clouds. Wet leaves glisten in the trees. Aunty May still isn't home. We've been to visit her a few times, and she looks so small and frail. It's strange to see her like that, helpless in bed. A month ago she was eighty years old and still chopping her own wood for the fire.

'I'm calling a family meeting,' Dave says.

I roll my eyes. Another famous Outhwaite family meeting. I reach down the bickie tin, hoping for Tim Tams, or at least some chocolate chip, but there are only some of Dave's dry, nuggety Anzacs.

I wonder if Adrian has told Dave and Olly that I'm not taking violin seriously. 'Let's have a family vote,' Dave will say. 'Should we keep wasting what precious little money we have on Else's violin lessons?'

But Dave isn't looking at me. He says, 'It's about my Aunt Dorothy. Your great-aunt.'

I breathe.

'You wouldn't remember her, any of you. Else is the only one who ever met her, at my parents' funeral.'

'After the car crash?' says Sibbi.

'Else was tiny, just a hairless possum wrapped in a blanket, like Hester was when we first met her.'

'Is she the same kind of aunty like Aunty May?' asks Sibbi.

'Aunty May is everybody's aunty,' says Olly, spreading her hands to include the neighbours, the people from the post office, the guys from the stock-and-feed shop. 'But Dorothy was just Daddy's aunty.'

Dave says, 'Anyway, we've had news that Aunt Dorothy died.'

I try to conjure a memory of myself and someone great-auntish, but all I can imagine is Aunty May holding Hester. Still, I feel some measure of importance, since I'm the only one who ever met Great-Aunt Dorothy.

Sibbi's eyes are round and worried. She's seen lots of dead things – kangaroos, wombats on the side of the road, flies with their legs in the air on the windowsills – yet she never takes it very well. Dave holds her hand.

'She was very elderly and she died in a hospice for old people. I looked it up online and it seemed very comfortable, very social. There was a choir, art classes. It wasn't a sad death, or a lonely death.'

'Did she have a long happy life?' asks Sibbi.

'Yes,' says Dave. 'I think she did. She never married, always lived in the same house. But she had lots of friends and did interesting work. She was some kind of scientist.

She worked with the BBC. She loved nature like Clancy. And Else, she was very fond of music. She would have loved to hear you play.'

At the thought of this, my chest grows tight again and the Anzac feels like sawdust in my mouth. I stand up. 'I should practise,' I say. 'Sorry about Aunt Dorothy.'

'Wait till Dad finishes,' Olly says.

I sigh, noisily, still standing. *Just get on with it.*

Dave continues. 'I was the only family she had left, I guess. Well, and you guys. She didn't like long-haul flying, and I meant to go and see her, maybe when you kids were older – it's so far and so expensive. We kept in touch after my parents died, Christmas cards mostly, I emailed her photos sometimes. I never really expected . . . well, I just didn't think about it.'

'What didn't you expect?' asks Oscar, looking as impatient as I felt.

'It turns out she's left me everything. The house. Some shares. Furniture. It's all a bit unclear at this stage.'

'Are we rich?' I ask.

'It's a joke,' says Oscar. 'Right?'

Dave shakes his head. 'It's not a joke. And I don't think we're rich exactly, there's a big inheritance tax we need to pay, but first we have to process the whole estate, and work out exactly *what* we've inherited. I can't really manage it all from here. So we're going to have to go over there.'

'Over where?' Finn asks.

'England,' I say faintly.

'London,' says Dave.

'Where Baby Prince George lives,' Sibbi supplies helpfully. 'And the pussycat and the Queen.'

My parents glance at each other. I know exactly what they're thinking. The twins will be all right, as long as they have each other. Sibbi, at four, is young enough to adapt – they won't be worried about Sibbi. And Clancy, well ... He might pine, he might suffer more than anyone, away from the animals and the bush, but he won't shout or get cross. He'll make things as easy as he can for everybody else.

It's me everyone turns to look at. I am the unknown quantity. I could stamp my foot, refuse to go. I probably couldn't stop them, but I could make it as unpleasant as possible. I feel oddly powerful, standing over them.

'What about Hester?' I say, finally. 'How can Clancy leave her?'

'She'll be all right,' Clancy says quietly. 'It's time she grew up, I guess.'

'What about Mum's uni?' I say. 'And your fences?'

I notice that Olly doesn't look as keen as Dave. 'I can write my thesis over there,' she says. 'I've already talked to my supervisor. I'll miss the teaching, but –' She breaks off, then adds as if it explains everything, 'We're a family.'

'Well, I won't miss building fences,' says Dave.

'I thought building fences was your passion,' I say.

After Sibbi was born, Dave gave up his job as a lawyer in the city. He said he wanted to do something honest with his hands, build something real instead of working overtime reading contracts and pushing papers around a desk to make a small handful of rich people even richer.

Dave shrugs. 'Turns out, not so much.'

I step back to the kitchen window. Aunty May's house is already in shadow. Night is creeping into the valley.

'What about Aunty May?' I ask, but of course no one can answer that. I know as well as Dave and Olly do that Aunty May probably won't come back home. She'll go to some kind of aged care place. I hope it's as nice as Aunt Dorothy's sounded.

'What about Else?' Clancy asks. 'What about her violin lessons?'

'We can find a teacher over there,' Olly says.

'It doesn't matter,' I say. The room seems to be swaying. I feel a sudden swoop in my belly, like I'm falling. I hold on to the bench to steady myself.

'Of course it matters,' Olly says.

'But it doesn't,' I say, wondering if it's true. 'It really doesn't. I'm fine.'

CLANCY

I LIE AWAKE in the dark, listening to Hester scramble on the roof. I test my feelings about the move.

Of course I'll miss Hester. But there will be new animals to learn about. Storybook animals: squirrels, moles, hedgehogs, otters. Badgers and weasels and shrews. Not in the city, though.

When I think about school, I feel only relief. I loved Christmas Hills Primary School. I'd been happy in that little school, only forty of us, and most years the twins were in the same class as me. But this year I've started at the high school in the suburbs, though it's so big that I hardly ever see Else except on the bus. Actually, I wouldn't mind school, if only it wasn't for lunchtime and recess. Why do they have to be so long?

And the bus ride home. It's okay if Else is on the bus too – then they pretty much leave me alone. But on the days Else has violin lessons . . .

Missy Carter and Keeley Smith and those girls. They confuse me, coming up to me one at a time, telling me they're sorry, that they just want to be friends. And I say it's fine. It's always a trick. I know it's a trick, but I don't know what else to say. While I'm distracted one of the girls eases my maths book or drink bottle out of my bag and passes it to the others, and then they start tossing it around. They always give it back, but not until I'm red in the face and almost crying.

Worse is when they do the same thing with my words, tricking me into saying something, like which one of them do I think is the nicest, or the smartest, or the best looking. Snatching my words and tossing them around until they're tattered and dirty and wrecked. Last week, Keeley reported me to the bus monitor, her big eyes swimming with real tears, for saying she's fat, which I don't think I said, but I'm not even sure myself anymore.

Hester scrabbles and slides on the tin roof, leaping up at the eucalyptus tree whose long branches sway low over the house. The rain begins again, a slow steady drum and then, I suppose, I fall asleep.

SIBBI

IN APRIL IN Christmas Hills, one day sweeps into another like dry leaves. It's cold outside. The air smells of woodsmoke and damp soil. The days are shortening. Sibbi and Hester know not to get underfoot. Clancy makes a nest for Hester in a wooden box. Sibbi helps him line it with the woollen jumper and he nails it under the eaves on the veranda.

'Is it comfy for Hester?' Sibbi asks.

'She has to learn to get used to us not being here,' Clancy tells her. 'That's the kindest way.'

In bed that night Sibbi unexpectedly weeps for Hester and can't be comforted, but Clancy does not cry.

Arrangements are made. Boxes are filled, rattling with cups and saucers, or bulging with books. Daddy puts a sign by the gate, *Permanent Garage Sale*, and Sibbi watches cars wend up the driveway, bringing neighbours and strangers to finger through Daddy's records or measure up chests of drawers. Daddy hums happily every time someone drives away with a car-boot stuffed with their belongings but Sibbi just watches.

They take a load of things to the op shop too, cramming it into the back of the van. 'You'll miss the van,' says Clancy. 'It's like your other child.'

'Our van?' says Sibbi.

'Rick's van now,' says Daddy.

Daddy's fence-building friend, Rick, has arranged to buy the van; on the last day he will drive them all to the airport and then he will drive away in it forever. Everything is fitting into place.

'When do you move?' the next-door neighbours ask. 'You lucky ducks.' They drive away with the Outhwaite's dining table strapped to the roof of their station wagon.

'Are we lucky?' Sibbi asks.

'Oh, yes,' says Mama. Her voice echoes, hollow in the stripped living room. With the dining table and couch gone, they'll have to eat picnic-style on the floor. Mama sighs. 'Very lucky.'

ELSE

THAT'S WHAT EVERYONE at school says too. 'You're so lucky.'

Well, except for poor lovely Sam, who looks miserable all the time. I avoid lovely Sam and his broken heart. I take shelter in the thick forest of girls, and comfort from the rituals of gossip.

At recess one day, late in April, a week before we're to leave, I sit in the autumn sun, thick as treacle, listening.

Kasey likes Logan.

'I don't *like* him,' Kasey protests. 'I *love* him.'

'Well, you like him *and* you love him,' Tilly says.

'Hm,' says Kasey. 'I'm not sure I like him all that much. He's a bit of a creep. But I can't help loving him.'

'That's not love,' says Camille. 'That's raw animal attraction.'

'Changing the subject,' says Kasey. She offers Camille a barbecue chip. Camille nibbles at it like a mouse, one crinkly ridge at a time, as Kasey offers the packet around.

The chip I draw out of the packet is folded over, curling into itself.

'A wish chip!' says Tilly. 'Make a wish.'

'I can't believe you aren't going to be here for my party,' Camille says to me, for the twentieth time.

I smile and shrug and crunch the chip, without making a wish.

Luce makes meaningful eye contact with Kasey – so subtle! – and then stands up. 'Come on, Tilly, Kase, let's go for a walk. Maybe Logan's playing soccer at the bottom oval.'

'Stay with me, Else,' says Camille. 'I'm going to miss you the most.' When the other girls are out of earshot, Camille tells me casually, 'You know how Luce has liked Sam for ages . . .'

No. I did not know that.

'Well, she has. But she stopped liking him, of course, when you started going out with him. Out of loyalty to you. But now you're going away, well. Luce was wondering, would you mind if she asked him to my party?'

I wonder if this is why Camille planned the party for after I leave instead of before.

'I mean, you're going away forever, yeah?' Camille says.

'Sam is a free agent,' I tell Camille.

I'm surprised to find that I can still breathe. Bodies are certainly efficient machines.

On the bus Clancy's gaggle of little girlfriends giggle and nudge each other. 'Which one of us are you going to miss most?' I hear one of them ask. Clancy blushes scarlet and mumbles something.

Our house is bare of most things. We are already living out of suitcases, using only the clothes, books and toys we're taking with us.

Sam calls the home phone almost the second I walk through the door. (I've had my mobile switched off all day.) 'Luce asked me to Camille's party,' he tells me.

'So?' I say. 'You should go.'

'If you were going to be here, I'd go with you.'

'But I'm not going to be.'

'Well, I don't want to go with Luce.'

When I hang up, Olly says, 'Poor Sam.'

'Yes,' I say, a little impatient. Everyone loves Sam. I sometimes think my family wonders what he sees in me. 'Poor Sam. Lovely Sam.'

Sibbi says, 'Is Lovely Sam coming to see me?'

I shake my head.

'But he loves me,' says Sibbi. 'And I love him.'

'He'll wait for you,' I say to Sibbi, 'if you ask him to.'

'You're only very young,' Olly tells Sibbi. 'No need to get serious now.'

'I know,' I say. 'That's what I told him.'

'I'm seriously serious,' says Sibbi.

I go into the bedroom that I share with Sibbi. Two open suitcases, two mattresses on the floor, and my violin. My music stand is set up in the same corner it's always been, and when I face it, the house behind me could be whole, with cupboards full of all the familiar, friendly objects we have owned all my remembering life, chipped mugs and water-rippled books and sea shells and candle stubs and the things that make a home.

I'm not sentimental, though. I've been more ruthless than anyone. I'd taken great pleasure in throwing things out, burning all my old schoolbooks and reports, my Year Seven and Eight diaries, the supernatural romance novels I was addicted to when I was twelve, paintings and drawings I did in primary school. At the last minute I decided I couldn't bear to burn Teddy Bill or Mousie or Baby Frank, so I gave them away to the op shop instead. I stuffed them into one of those charity bins and walked away without looking back. Sibbi howled. '*I* love Mousie. *I* love Teddy Bill. *I* love Baby Frank,' she wailed and wailed, and when she came home she was so angry with me she buried my phone in the back yard. The phone still works, except that when I call anyone they sound like they're underwater. But I don't know anyone to call in England anyway, and it will be too expensive to call my friends back home. We'll keep in touch the old-fashioned way: email.

Sibbi's rage only pushed me further, cleaning out my wardrobe. In the end I kept hardly anything: some summer clothes, a few pairs of winter jeans, my boots. Nothing for sentimental reasons. We'll have to buy proper winter clothes once we're there anyway, Dave and Olly said, for proper winters.

I like the idea of living lean. Borrowing books rather than buying them, discarding clothes as the seasons pass, living free of keepsakes and clutter. Not hanging on to the relics of my past. Not hoarding things for the future. Light enough to travel anywhere.

Poor lovely Sam. Have I given him away too? *I mean,* Camille's voice echoes in my head, *you're going away forever, yeah?*

I lift the violin to my chin. The notes stagger and stumble, trip and fail.

The Mozart. The Mozart. The Mozart.

SIBBI

ONE DAY SIBBI wakes up and it's the last proper day in Australia.

Oscar and Finn spend it saying things like:

'This time tomorrow Rick will be driving us to the airport.'

'This time tomorrow we'll be in the departure lounge.'

'This time tomorrow we'll be on the plane. Will we have taken off yet? Yes. Now we'll be flying over Queensland, Papua New Guinea, Indonesia.'

But for Sibbi it is a day of last times.

At breakfast: 'Is this the last pear I will eat from our trees?' she asks.

'Definitely,' says Daddy. 'The birds ate the rest.'

At the post office: 'Is this the last time we'll get the mail?' she asks. Daddy squeezes her hand.

'Oh,' says Mei-Ling behind the counter. 'We'll miss you!' She gives Sibbi a Caramello Koala, and, after a moment, with tears in her eyes, gives Daddy one too.

And later with Mama: 'This is the last time we are walking down the track. This is the last time we are feeding the chook chook chooks. This is the last time we are fetching the eggies.' The hens regard Sibbi with baleful eyes as Sibbi reaches into their little house for two brown eggs.

'Yes,' says Mama. 'Shall we take the eggies to the Marshes? We won't have a chance to eat them before tomorrow. We'll have to ask the Marshes to look after Aunty May's chook chook chooks.'

When it comes time to say goodbye to the Marshes, Sibbi grows uncharacteristically shy and buries her head in Mama's side and sucks her fingers, a habit she has almost (but not quite) grown out of.

As they walk down the Marshes' driveway, Mama stops and looks across at the hills, and breathes in a deep breath. 'I feel a bit homesick already, Sibbi,' she says.

Sibbi takes Mama's hand. 'Can you really get sick of home?' Sibbi asks.

'Sick *for* home. Oh, it's not a real sickness, Sibbi. More like a sadness.'

'I feel homesad already too.'

'I suppose London will *be* our home,' says Mama. 'Isn't that funny?'

Sibbi doesn't answer. It is not funny. She has a feeling about London that is too big to name. Every day the feeling gets a little bit bigger, and now it is taking up so much room inside her body it feels like there is no room left for anything else, maybe not even enough room for Sibbi.

CLANCY

I SPEND THE last day roaming my territory, followed by the Davidsons' black-and-white collie, Spider. Up to the back paddocks we go, and over the Marshes' land, where the old white horse comes up for a nuzzle and an apple core. The kangaroos look up, then go back to their grazing as if I'm as much a part of the hill as the kangaroos themselves, or the sulphur-crested cockatoos, who shriek and swing in the dead branches of an old gum tree, loving themselves sick.

Spider and I sit down by the creek, swollen by autumn rains. Spider seems to realise this is a solemn occasion, because he doesn't go looking for a fallen branch or piece of washed-up fence paling for me to throw. He sits quietly, his body pressed against me. Coloured parrots flicker in the trees. I reach out my hand and rest it on the ruff of his neck.

'Almost time to go, old man,' I say.

But we sit, just a little longer.

ELSE

I STAY AWAY. I spend my last days with my friends. I sleep at Audrey's house one night, and Camille's house the next. We all catch the train in to the big suburban shopping mall and wander around the shops. We eat dumplings at the Teahouse. We see a movie, though I can't remember anything about it later. I try to make everything as normal as possible, as if I'm just going on a quick trip to Tasmania or New Zealand, like the other girls do over Easter.

'Wow, you're being so cool about it,' says Kasey. 'I'd be freaking out if I were you.'

'Imagine,' says Camille, as she spoons cappuccino froth into her mouth. 'You'll be so close to Europe. Paris. Milan. Think of the fashion. Think of the shoes!'

I try to smile, try to look as excited as they do. I look at Camille's white tee and pale jeans offset with a bulky mustard-coloured scarf and chunky boots, Audrey's neat fifties-style dress and cardigan and ballet flats, Kasey in her black jeggings, oversized hoodie and scuffed Cons, Tilly with her jeans and

Blundstones covered in paint splashes. What will the girls be like in London? What will they wear? What will they talk about? What will they think of me?

'Shoes?' scoffs Tilly. 'What about the music, the art, the history?'

I rub an invisible spot on my Doc Marten boot with my thumb.

We walk out the front of the shopping centre, where Olly is waiting in the van. Audrey gives me an envelope. 'From all of us.'

'Should I open it now?'

'Later.'

'I'll only be an email away,' I say. 'Send me photos of the party.'

I step up into the passenger seat, and wind the window down.

Audrey wipes away tears and leans her head on Tilly's shoulder.

'Aussie Aussie Aussie!' Camille shouts, as Olly revs the engine. 'Oi oi oi!'

Kasey chases the van down the street, waving both arms as Olly drives us away, honking the horn. When Kasey gets to the corner she keeps leaping up and down, still waving. I blow kisses out the window until I can't see them anymore.

'They're such great girls,' Olly sighs.

'Don't,' I snap.

I lean back against the seat and open the envelope. Inside is a card they have all signed and a ticket to a Mozart festival at the Albert Hall in July.

Olly stops to pick up fish and chips on the way home. We drive the winding road, the paper packet steaming on my lap. We turn at Aunty May's dark cottage to chug up the driveway towards the house on the hill. 'This is the –' I stop myself.

'I know,' says Olly. 'The last time we'll be coming home.'

Our whole family sits on the lounge-room floor. We open the paper parcels of fish and chips. We don't even worry about plates. We eat with our hands, licking the salty grease from our fingers.

'This time tomorrow we'll be eating dinner on the plane,' says Oscar.

'Our house will be lonely of us,' says Sibbi. 'Do houses get people-sick?'

'Thank you, house,' says Olly. She cups her mouth and calls up, as if the listening spirit of the house resides somewhere in the ceiling. 'Thank you! Thank you for the shelter. Thank you for the dreams. Thanks for all the days and nights.'

It's desperately cringe-y, but I feel slow and sleepy, full of fish and chips, and I'm glad she says it.

'Thanks for the music,' says Dave. 'Thanks for the peace and quiet. Thanks for the noise.'

'The house is listening,' says Sibbi. 'The house says thank you too.'

The last wood burns in the fire. The pobblebonks twang in the dam outside. Hester scrabbles on the roof. A tawny frogmouth hoo-hoos deeply nearby. Sibbi starts to fall asleep in Dave's arms. There's no telly to watch, and the books we are taking with us are packed tightly into our carry-on bags. But no one feels like going to bed. Olly, Clancy and the twins,

Sibbi and even me, we drag our mattresses into the living room. We camp one last night near the fire, lying side by side in the small house that has been home to us for years, the only home that Sibbi has ever known.

One by one, we drift off to sleep, until only I am awake, listening to the pop and crackle of the fire, like the house is talking to itself.

ELSE

I PRESS MY head against the window of the van and feel the gentle thrum of the engine vibrate through my skull. I watch as we travel through the gently winding country roads and green hills, then the strip malls and the strange new housing estates and service stations, until we hit the freeway and there is nothing to see but trucks, cars, grey road, grey sky.

As Rick pulls the van into the airport carpark, I touch my heel gently to my violin case. Bending to pick up my backpack, I shove the violin back under the seat. I'm the last out of the van. By the time I get out, Olly has already entered the airport, dragging a wheely case behind her, Sibbi hoisted on one hip. Dave and the boys rush to keep up. I follow at a leisurely pace.

'Want me to carry your bag?' Rick asks.

He's not that much older than me. He's bought the van to travel around Australia. I think about what that would be like, just getting in a car behind a steering wheel and pointing it in any direction you want.

'No thanks,' I say. 'It's not heavy.' My backpack feels so light, my hands completely free. No one seems to notice that I've left my violin in the van.

Olly and Dave rummage through bags, gathering the passports and tickets. Every time they look up, one of us has disappeared.

Dave finds Sibbi by the plastic life-sized guide dog, petting it gently and whispering something in his ear.

He finds Clancy, who originally set out to look for Sibbi, gazing into a poster warning of the demise of the Borneo rainforests. Orang-utans stare soulfully back at Clancy.

The twins play a game of queue tiggy with each other, ducking and weaving, much to the amusement and consternation of fellow passengers. I wait to one side, trying to look like I'm heading off overseas on my own adventure, a young backpacker. I'm angry with Olly and Dave (probably unfairly, I'm mostly angry with Olly) for not noticing the absence of my violin.

'You could help,' Olly snaps at me, grabbing Finn on his way past and holding him tight.

'If you'd asked *my* opinion,' I say, 'you could have stopped at one child and saved yourself a lot of bother.'

'Thanks very much,' says Finn.

'Come on, Else,' says Olly. 'Just a little consideration.'

'Why am *I* in trouble? They're the ones running around!'

The woman at the counter calls, 'Next!' and looks overwhelmed as Olly hands over seven passports.

Finally we have our boarding passes and the big cases are checked in. We make our way towards the International

Departure Lounge. Suddenly I see a group of smiling familiar faces. There is something shocking about these faces being here, in the alien environs of the airport, with its gleaming tile floors and fluorescent lighting.

There's Rick, the Marshes, Kasey and her mum (who is also a close friend of Olly's), Mr Park, the principal of the primary school, who has taught all us Outhwaite kids, and heaps of Dave and Olly's other friends: Kaime the fire twirler, Odette the sad poet, Alexei who cuts our hair and knows all the local gossip, Shane who owns the wood-fired pizza restaurant. Even Nan and Pop are there, looking older, and smaller, and as disapproving as ever.

Oh, and Sam! Poor Sam, lovely Sam. He peels himself away from the group.

'What are you doing here?' I say.

'I've come to say goodbye,' he says. His black curls bob down into his dark eyes.

'Fine,' I say, slapping him gently on the arm. 'Bye, then.'

But he hugs me tight, and I bury my face into his shirt, letting it absorb the dampness from my eyes. I count backwards from ten and when I pull away I have regained control.

'Where's your violin?' he asks.

'Checked it in,' I lie.

'Are you sure that's a good idea? Haven't you ever watched the baggage handlers throwing stuff into the plane?'

I haven't. But it's typical that Sam has. 'Bye, Sam,' I say.

'You'll miss me,' he says.

'Not as much as you'll miss me.'

I look around. Everybody is laughing and crying at the same time. Everybody is hugging everybody, saying *goodbye* and *stay in touch* and *come home soon* and *safe travels and take care* until Sibbi puts her hands on her ears, opens her mouth wide and screams.

Pop frowns. 'We'd better start driving back, Nance,' he says, and adds, 'You don't get as much mileage to the gas as you used to, I think they water it down,' to no one in particular. Poor old Pop. It's so strange to think warm, loving, chaotic Olly came from such a tightly wound, reserved couple as Nan and Pop.

'We'd better head through customs,' says Dave.

'It was nice of you all to come and see us off,' says Olly, and she and Dave gather the other kids in front of them. Sam puts an arm around me, kisses the top of my head, and whispers something into my hair that I don't quite catch.

We pass through the doors into the area restricted to ticket holders only. It's suddenly very quiet. The silence is like a pressure on my ears.

There are more queues in Customs and another game of queue tiggy until Dave roars, 'Everybody! SIT down!' The boys stop running, at least.

Sibbi starts to sob. 'What's wrong?' asks Olly.

'Daddy made me cry.'

Olly rubs her temples.

SIBBI

AFTER THE WAITING and the boredom, getting on the plane is a relief. Sibbi is fascinated by the blankets and pillows on the seats; the drawstring bags containing eye masks, socks, toothpaste and toothbrushes; the televisions in the seat backs.

Oscar, Finn, Clancy and Dave sit in four seats in the middle of the plane. Sibbi, Mama and Else sit in a bank of three.

Mama gives Else the window seat. 'Nice to see Sam?' she asks Else, trying to make amends. Else grunts and looks out the window.

'I don't want Mama,' says Sibbi. 'I want Daddy.'

Mama leans over and calls to Daddy. They get up, and rearrange themselves. Daddy settles himself into the seat and does up his seatbelt.

'Are we going to see Aunty May now?' asks Sibbi.

'No,' says Daddy, with forced patience. 'We're on the plane. To England.'

'But I want to see Aunty May.'

'We talked about this. You said you didn't want to go and see her again in the hospital because it was too sad.'

'But I do want to. I change-ded my minds.'

'We can't, sweetie. It's too late.'

'It's not too late. I want to see Aunty May. I want to see Aunty May *now*.' Sibbi kicks her legs.

'Don't kick the back of the seat, sweetie,' Daddy says.

'I want Mama.'

'Sibbi, this is ridiculous,' says Daddy. 'We're not switching seats again.'

Sibbi draws a big breath.

'Here we go,' says Else.

'Mama!' Sibbi wails. 'MAH-MA.'

Daddy and Mama switch seats again.

'I'm going to have to ask you to put your seatbelt on,' the flight attendant scolds Mama as Mama stuffs her bag back under the seat.

Finally, finally, the journey begins.

ELSE

THE PLANE RISES above the runway and the airport, over the green hills of the outer suburbs. The city, which I've mostly seen from the hills on the outskirts, always looking like something from a dark fairytale, tall towers poking sharply at the sky, looks completely different from up here in the air, small as matchsticks, like the dioramas we made in grade six.

I try to make out the route home, try to locate which green hill is – was – ours, but I cannot imagine belonging to that miniature world below. It's as if it's already a story of a place I once lived, and not the place itself at all.

Soon enough we fly up into a bank of clouds, and the city disappears altogether.

The flight attendants bring along an early dinner. Olly opens all the little packages for Sibbi, pasta with meat sauce, a bread roll, juice, biscuits and cheese. Sibbi has a bite of the bread roll and refuses everything else.

'There's nothing here I like,' she whimpers.

'Don't be silly,' says Olly. 'You love pasta. Look, crackers with cheese. Yum yum.'

Sibbi pushes the tray away, almost upsetting everything onto Olly's lap.

'At least finish the bread. Has she eaten anything today?' Olly asks me.

I roll my eyes. 'How should *I* know?'

Typical, I think, of Olly not to notice what her children *have* or *haven't* done.

And then I'm feeling a bit queasy myself. What will Olly and Dave say when they realise I've left a perfectly good, perfectly *expensive* violin in the van. And not by accident either. On *purpose*? What will Rick think when he finds it wedged under the back seat?

I send my tray back, almost untouched, with Sibbi's.

SIBBI

HONG KONG IS colour and noise and smells. The steamy fragrance of noodle houses; the chemical floral of perfume; the sweetness of the French-Asian bakeries; the savoury tang of salty dried fish; plasticky wafts of pollution, and nasal humidity. Hong Kong is city skylines, sparkling harbour, distant jade hills, traffic-stained apartment buildings, bright shining commerce and stuffed, shabby stores, and people, so many people.

Mama wants to see the bird garden, but Clancy refuses. Else loses an argument to explore the city on her own. Sibbi refuses to go anywhere without Mama.

'We'll split up then,' says Daddy. 'I'll take the boys, you take the girls.'

Mama urges Sibbi, who has been on a hunger strike since the plane, to eat. But Sibbi eyes fried yellow balls of pastry, dried fish, chicken feet hanging up on display, rambutan, loquats, and keeps her mouth closed. She shakes her head *no* at everything, even familiar food like yoghurt and bananas.

Mama tries to keep hold of Sibbi's hand, but Sibbi squirms

and protests, first running ahead, then dragging behind, stopping to look at a living wall of goldfish in inflated plastic bags and to touch flowers in a plastic bucket. Else strides ahead, ignoring Mama's calls to wait.

The bird market is walled. They go through the moongate into the garden, divided by archways into courtyards. The sound of birds, clucking, fluttering, wittering, whistling, chirping and squawking fills the singing air and the city seems suddenly far away. Ornate bird cages hang from hooks above them and in each one is a single bird, little chests rising and falling.

There are stacked plastic crates and wire cages on the ground, overcrowded with birds. These ones are for sale. The single birds in the pretty cages are pets, out for the air, and for their owners to sit together, smoking and socialising.

It is a shock to Sibbi to see a pink and grey galah in a metal cage. It's so familiar, a part of her everyday landscape, but belongs to the green hills of home/not-home.

Sibbi stops to look at tiny blue and silver bird in a bamboo cage on a stool, at her eye level. The elderly man who owns it shuffles up, hooks the cage on a long stick and hangs it high overhead.

Sibbi, who has been on the verge of angry tears all morning, howls with disappointment and rage. Mama tries to catch the eye of the man with the bird, wondering if she can somehow explain, convince him to bring it down again, but he shuffles away with surprising vigour.

Mama leads Sibbi away. Sibbi scratches and fights, then collapses on the ground, pressing her forehead to a stone bench, sobbing.

ELSE

IT'S ONLY WHEN Sibbi starts screaming that I notice,
suddenly, what a male space the bird market is. There are
women working in the stalls, but they are very much in
the background, behind all the stacked plastic crates. The
majority of people in the garden, sitting, hanging out with
their pet birds, are men. I feel like the worst kind of tourist,
ignorant, intruding on something I don't understand.

'I want to see the bird!' wails Sibbi.

'Can't you control your children?' I snap at Olly.

'Hey, that's not fair.' Olly looks on the verge of tears herself.

'Sibbi,' I hiss. 'Shut up. Stop screaming.'

'Else, for goodness sake. You're making it worse,' says Olly.

'How am *I* making it worse?'

'Just let her cry it out. She's tired and hungry.'

'I'm not ti-i-ired.'

'Why are we moving to England?' I demand. 'Dad's the
one who inherited the house. Why do we all have to go?
Nobody asked me if I want to uproot my whole life.'

'Do you really think this is the time?'

'Yes, I do,' I say, even though I know I am tired and hungry too. But the anger I've felt since leaving the violin in the van burns through my blood.

'There's lots of birds,' Olly says to Sibbi. 'So many birds. Lookit all the birds.'

'I don't want lotsa birds! I want *that* bird!'

'I've had to give up *everything*. My friends. My boyfriend. My school. It's too much to ask. It's not fair.'

'It's too late. I can't fix it,' says Olly, but is she talking to me or to Sibbi? 'Come on,' she urges Sibbi. 'Let's go find another bird.'

'No! No other bird!'

'I think I'm old enough to have a say in my own life.'

'Do you think I want to go to England?' Olly howls suddenly, spinning to face me. 'I'm giving up stuff too. *My* friends. *My* uni. *My* work. Did you think about that?'

I falter. It hadn't really occurred to me that Olly might not want to go to England. 'Well, why are we going then?'

'Because! We're a family! And we love each other! All right?'

Olly swoops, scoops up Sibbi and hauls her screaming out of the gardens, not looking back to see if I'm following. I feel the gaze of the men and their birds, and though part of me wants to disappear forever into the noise and colour of Hong Kong, I rush to catch up with Olly.

Dave and the boys are lying on beds in the hotel room, flicking through manga comics. Dave looks shocked at the dishevelled mess of me, Olly and Sibbi as we collapse into the room.

Olly deposits Sibbi into Dave's arms. 'I'm going out,' she says, and she does, the door slamming closed behind her.

Sibbi is inconsolable.

'What on earth –?' Dave asks me.

I shake my head. 'Don't even.'

'Shall I go and look for Mum?' Clancy asks.

'She'll be back soon,' says Dave, hopefully. 'Let's just calm things down a notch.'

Calming things down a notch means finding American cartoons on the television.

Olly does come back. She has hot pho, dumplings, and a huge container of soft white rice for Sibbi, which Sibbi eats with her hands.

'I was sad,' Sibbi says.

'Yes. You were sad,' says Olly. 'You were cross.'

'I'm happy now!' says Sibbi. 'Are you cross, Mama?'

'Nope,' says Olly.

I am not cross either. I think of the little bird, the bird Sibbi broke her heart over. I think about the old man who didn't want to share his bird, hanging the cage up high, so a little girl could no longer see it. I think about him walking home at the end of the day, carrying his bird in its narrow cage. And I think of him in one of those thousands of greasy windowed apartments in Mongkok, in the pollution-stained streets, eating his bowl of soupy noodles, all alone with his caged bird.

ALMOST ANNIE
AND HARDLY ALICE

THE LONDON HOUSE has been shut up for weeks. The windows are flung open, the stale air of the house is replaced by a fresh, floral-scented spring breeze. Everything is dusted and vacuumed and scrubbed. Beds are made.

'So many beds!' says Almost Annie.

'Antipodeans,' sniffs Hardly Alice. 'I heard one of the cleaners say so.'

'Family,' says Almost Annie. 'The little nephew. I remember him. Such a funny, sweet boy.'

'Was he?'

'You never remember anything.'

'He'll be a grown-up man now, anyway.'

'With children of his own.'

'Hundreds, by the look of it. Colonials overrunning the house. What will become of us?'

'The master bedroom,' counts Almost Annie. 'That will be the parents. Three beds upstairs, two in one room, one in the other. Two more on the middle floor.'

'Both in the big room. Dorothy's study is fit for neither man nor beast.'

'But when?' asks Almost Annie, thinking of all those made-up beds.

'Soon,' says Hardly Alice.

Soon, says an airy whistle through the house. *Soon.*

Soon, says a whisper, in the hidden room at the top of the house, a whisper like insect wings rasping together. *Soon*, says the thing that is made of darkness and forgetting, that is lost, so lost it is only the *feeling* of being lost. *Soon.*

ELSE

'How much longer, Mama?' Sibbi asks.

'Soon,' says Olly. I listen to the constant hum of the plane, pulling us further away from Hong Kong, and even further away from home. I don't know how long I've been drifting in and out of sleep – never quite asleep or quite awake – when the lights come back on again. Rays of rising sun stream through the windows and breakfast trays are handed out. The seatbelt lights come on. I wish the artificial twilight of the plane could last a bit longer. The plane descends through a bank of clouds and the English countryside sparkles below.

'It's so green!' I say. The storybook world – *Wind in the Willows, The Faraway Tree, Harry Potter, Peter Pan, Peter Rabbit, Watership Down, Jane Eyre, Pride and Prejudice* – is laid out below. Dense, iridescent, improbable green. A different sort of beauty from the rumpled grey eucalyptus, red clay dirt and yellow-green grass we've left behind. This is a closely cultivated beauty, as if every square centimetre has been tended by human hands.

I feel an unexpected thrill as the city forms below me, an amazing clockwork of tight streets, rows of identical houses. Clancy clutches the armrests at the grinding sound of the landing gear preparing for touchdown. As the plane lands, I hear Oscar ask Dave, 'So, when are we going back to Australia?'

Olly plays 'Round and round the garden' on Sibbi's palm.

Clancy closes his eyes but I keep mine wide open.

'Well, we're here,' says Dave as the runway rushes towards us. 'Welcome to England.'

CLANCY

THE PUBLIC BUS from Heathrow to Gunnersby is full, but Mum tells us it goes straight past the house on Mortlake Road, so we pile on. The twins and I squeeze into a double seat. Else heads up the back to sit on her own.

Jetlag makes everything look flat and sort of magical, like the figures and the houses are pictures cut out and stuck on a blue sky background. I try to work out what time it is in Australia, but I can't remember if we are ten hours ahead or behind. Would I normally be in bed by now? Sitting down to dinner or breakfast?

I've seen London on TV, in movies and read about it in books so many times, that seeing it in real life feels like a dream I've had before but can barely recall. Insubstantial, strange and familiar, all at once.

Along the wide pavement, a young mother pushes a very elegant, old-fashioned pram that looks straight out of *Mary Poppins*.

'Is that Princess Kate and Baby Prince George?' Sibbi asks, pointing at the lady and the pram.

'I don't think so,' says Dad, glancing up from the map on his phone. He is tracing our progress so we don't miss the stop.

'That pram would have cost more than our van back home,' Mum says.

'Is everyone in London rich?' asks Sibbi.

'I suppose not,' says Mum, though she sounds doubtful. All the houses seem rather grand, the streets clean and leafy.

'This is a fairly well-to-do area,' says Dad.

'Do you remember it at all?' Mum asks him.

'I wasn't much older than Sibbi when I lived in London,' says Dad. 'I remember some things, like double-decker buses. And I think there's a big park around here somewhere. I remember there were deer in it, just living wild.'

'Deer?' I ask, perking up.

'Yes. Like mobs of kangaroos at home. Fairly tame I suppose. Urban deer.'

'Urban deer!' Finn snorts. 'That sounds like they have beards and black-rimmed glasses and drink flat whites and upload selfies on Instagram.'

'Huh?' says Oscar, opening his eyes for a minute. 'I don't get it.'

'Hipster deer,' I say. Oscar shrugs and shakes his head, then closes his eyes again.

'Did you live here, Mama?' Sibbi asks.

Mum shakes her head. 'No,' she says. 'I've never lived anywhere but Australia.'

'Me either,' says Sibbi.

The bus turns a corner and the houses get wider and grander, each one set apart from the next, with garden walls and large trees.

The street narrows a little and bends, and then Dad says, 'Here we are,' and presses the button to signal the bus to stop.

'Come on,' Mum says. She calls back to Else, 'We're getting off here.'

Mum lets Dad and Sibbi pass, then heaves the backpack on her back, and tugs the wheely case behind her. We move towards the door.

'Look at all those children!' I hear a woman announce to her companion in a too-loud voice, and in a rather nasty way, as if she were saying, *Look at all those rodents!*

Mum tugs the case, which is stuck. She swears, trying to pull it free. For a moment, she looks like she might cry. I help her lift it free. Everyone else sits and stares at us. No one offers to help.

ALMOST ANNIE
AND HARDLY ALICE

ALMOST ANNIE STANDS at the window. She lifts her hand and waves.

'The family have arrived,' she says. 'Come and look.'

Hardly Alice lies on her back, her hands by her side, palms turned upwards. It is a yoga position she learned from watching Aunt Dorothy, called the corpse pose. She finds it very relaxing.

'Goody,' she says. She does not look.

ELSE

'THIS IS IT,' says Dave. 'Outhwaite House.'

We all gaze up at the enormous house – three or four storeys high, I'm too tired to count all the windows properly – looming over us.

Dave rummages in his backpack, looking for the set of keys from Mr Brompton.

The twins jostle each other in a tired, complaining sort of way, not a fight exactly and not exactly not a fight. Clancy sits on the garden wall. I perch beside him.

Dave checks his pockets again. 'You must have them,' he says to Olly.

'I don't have them. I never had them. Here, let me look.' Olly steps up onto the veranda and takes the backpack.

'Did Daddy lose the keys?' asks Sibbi.

'Hey!' says Clancy suddenly. 'Where's your violin?'

'Shh,' I hiss.

'Did you leave it on the plane?'

'Be quiet! If you must know, I left it in the van.'

'Well, that was stupid.'

I make a rude face.

'Wait, did you do it on purpose?'

'Are you going to tell on me? Because if you do . . .'

'Don't get your knickers in a knot. You know I never tell. But why on earth did you do it? Mum and Dad are going to kill you!'

'Shush,' I say again, but not so harshly this time. 'They'll hear you.'

All I want is to get into this new house, have a shower, something to eat and a sleep, not necessarily in that order. Tears prick my eyes.

'You duffer,' says Clancy, not unkindly, as if he is the big brother and I the little sister. 'Why do you have to make everything so hard for yourself?'

'Success!' calls Olly, holding up the bundle of keys. She tosses them to Dave.

'Here goes nothing,' he says. 'Let's hope there isn't a family of rats in the kitchen.'

'Bats in the belfry,' says Finn.

'Skeletons in the closet,' says Oscar.

'Shall we turn back now?' Dave asks Olly.

'No!' the twins and Sibbi shout, clamouring at the door as Dave turns the key in the lock. Clancy and I stand back, side by side.

'I wonder what it's like,' says Clancy. We don't have to wonder much longer.

The door opens. The twins are the first across the threshold. Then Dave and Sibbi. Olly reaches back a hand, and

Clancy takes it. I watch them all disappear into the house. The air on the street smells of honeysuckle and the promise of summer. The house smells of furniture polish and shadows and the past.

I pick up my bag, and follow them all inside.

SIBBI

THE TWINS BOLT up the stairs.

Mama drops the bags and gazes dazed around the spacious entryway. Even though it's quite bright and warm outside, between showers, inside the hallway it's dim and chilly.

'Come and explore the house, Mum,' Clancy says, tugging Mama's sleeve.

Mama shivers. 'Tea first,' she says. 'I'll find the kettle.'

Daddy stands in the hallway staring first at one painting and then another, generations of Outhwaites gazing down from the walls. 'Woah,' he says. 'I remember this. The carpet, the wallpaper . . . it's just the same as it was when I was a little boy. I thought I'd forgotten but it's all come rushing back.'

Sibbi stands in the hallway too, peering up the stairs. There were no stairs in the cottage on the hill.

She is down and Mama and Daddy are down and Else and Clancy and Finn and Oscar are up, up, up. She wants to go up with the boys and Else, but the stairs will carry her away from Mama and Daddy. She stands at the bottom of the staircase gazing upwards for a long time, listening to the sound of the twins calling out to each other from different rooms in the house.

Your brain is in your head, and your head is at the top of your body. Your blood flows all through your body, out of your heart and into your brain. Up up up. Your brain is your thought. Your brain is your mind and your mind is where you think. Sibbi thinks, *I am Sibbi.* Up up up.

'Shall we go and find your bedroom?'

'It's up the top,' says Sibbi. 'In the highest high room of the tall, tall house.'

'Hm,' says Daddy. 'I don't think so.'

'The house thinks so. The house says so.'

'I think you'll be sharing with Else for a while, till we're all settled in. Just up this first flight of stairs.'

Sibbi is pleased about sharing with Else. She takes her Daddy's hand and together, they climb the stairs.

ELSE

'I KNOW WHAT an endsister is,' Sibbi says as Olly tucks her into bed.

'Hmm?' Olly murmurs.

'It's a kind of a ghost.'

'Is it?' I can tell Olly is not really listening, but I shiver underneath the sheets.

Sibbi often says spooky things, and I don't always pay much attention, but here in the new, strange house, Sibbi's words seem to have shadows.

Olly said months ago it's because Sibbi is Oedipal, though I don't really get what that means.

'On the cusp between knowing and not knowing about life's mysteries. Teetering at the edge of the abyss,' Olly explained, cryptically. She was writing her thesis at the time, caught somewhere between the real world of our family and the inner world of her deep thinking. At sixteen I don't understand life's mysteries yet, so I don't really see how Sibbi could be so close to them.

'I know what an endsister is,' says Sibbi again.

We are endsisters, I think, *Sibbi and I*. Bookends, oldest and youngest, with the three boys sandwiched in between.

'We don't believe in ghosts,' I say. 'Do we, Mum?'

'Don't we?' says Olly, distracted. She focuses. 'Oh, no. I suppose not.'

'I don't see why I have to go to bed at the same time as the baby,' I complain, though my head spins woozily from lack of sleep.

'I'm not a baby,' Sibbi protests.

'That's right,' Olly says. 'You're my big girl.'

'I'm not a big girl!'

'Oh,' says Olly. 'What are you?'

'I'm Sibbi.'

'Fair enough,' says Olly. 'That's quite profound, really.'

'I can't believe we've inherited a mansion, and I still have to share a room.'

Olly sighs. 'We'll think about sleeping arrangements, I promise. But this will have to work for now.'

Actually, I'm glad I don't have to sleep alone in this big, creaky, creepy house. But I'm not about to admit this to Olly, or to Sibbi.

'Goodnight, girls. I'll be just upstairs if you need me.'

Just upstairs is an unfathomable distance. Sibbi knows it. I know it.

'Do you like our new house?' Sibbi asks me.

'Hm,' I say. 'I don't know. Do you?'

Sibbi yawns. 'This house likes me. But I don't like the *other* room.'

'What other room? There's hundreds of rooms. Do you mean the formal lounge? The one with the stuffed deer head?'

'No,' says Sibbi. 'I mean the Other-room. She doesn't like it either.'

'Who? Mama?'

'No,' says Sibbi, rolling over and cuddling into the pillow. 'That girl there, watching us sleep.'

'Where?' I sit up in bed. 'There's no one there.'

'She wented away just when you looked.' Sibbi yawns again.

'Ri-i-ight.' I lie back down. 'Go to sleep, Sibbi.'

'I am asleep.'

'Goodnight, Sibbi.'

'I am goodnight.'

Sleep descends like a wave.

ELSE

I WAKE UP after a long, dreamless night, still exhausted. The morning is already progressing without me. Sibbi's bed is empty.

I go downstairs. My parents are in the kitchen, sitting at the large oak table with a man Dave introduces as Mr Brompton.

'I was just telling your parents, Elspbeth, that I've been throwing myself at the problem of schools, and where you and your brothers might go come September – your parents are quite right, no point starting this late in the year. Oh, and the little girl, of course.'

'Sibbi's going to school?' I ask Olly.

Olly shrugs. 'Apparently they start at four here.'

'You mean like kindergarten?'

Olly shakes her head. 'More like prep. School shoes and everything, Mr Brompton says.'

I open my mouth to say how *stupid* that is, but then I see how miserable Olly and Dave look.

'Yes, yes,' says Mr Brompton. 'All right and proper. Wouldn't want the little one to languish uneducated now, would we?' But he says it kindly enough. He turns his attention back to me. 'Now, as it happens, it would appear you have a choice to make. We've found two schools with a place for you. I made some notes. Here we go. Kingsley Comprehensive is a co-ed school with a strong –' He peers over his glasses, frowning at his own handwriting. 'Arts and humanities focus. There's a brochure here.'

The brochure has a photo of the school chamber group on the cover. They are dressed like any school chamber group, in neat grey uniforms, perhaps a little scruffy at the edges. In fact, they could all be students of the school I just left behind in Australia.

'That looks great,' says Olly, a little too enthusiastically.

'I suppose. What's the other one?'

'The other is the Lady Emily Hartington School for Girls. This is Miss Dorothy Outhwaite's old stomping ground, as it were, and she' remained a loyal Old Girl of the school, er, financially speaking. They'd be happy to have you, and there's an Old Girl's scholarship they suggest may suit. It's usually reserved for direct descendants – children, grandchildren – but in this case they're happy to make an exception.'

I take that brochure. These girls look nothing like anyone I've ever known.

'And it's a good school too?' Olly asks.

'One of the oldest in London. Yet quite progressive, I am given to understand. Very strong in the sciences. I seem to remember there was an article about their new robotics lab in the newspaper recently.'

'What do you reckon, Else?' Olly says.

'There's no contest, is there? She'll got to Kingsley,' Dave says. 'I mean, no offence to Lady Penelope, but –'

'Hang on a minute,' I say, annoyed.

'Come on,' Dave laughs. 'You? At an uppity girls school?'

'Kingsley does sound like a good fit,' Olly agrees. 'The other school, the Lady Jane whatsit . . .'

'Lady Emily Hartington,' Mr Brompton supplies.

'Come on, Else. A private school?' Olly says. 'Hats and blazers? You'd hate it.'

'We will need to finalise the issue in reasonable haste,' says Mr Brompton. 'Of course you might like to tour the schools first?'

'She'll go to Kingsley,' says Dave.

'No, I won't!' I mean that I won't automatically go to Kingsley, that it's my decision, but it comes out as if I am firmly in favour of Lady Emily Hartington.

'But what about your music?' says Olly. 'Kingsley sounds really promising. It's co-ed, it has an arts focus, it doesn't cost the earth . . .'

'Mr Brompton says there's a scholarship for Lady Jane Whatsit.'

'Lady Emily Hartington,' says Dave. 'Whoever she is when she's at home. It sounds like a finishing school. Maybe you'll learn to walk in high heels with a tea tray on your head.'

'Awesome,' I say, flatly.

Olly sighs. 'That's a bit sexist, Dave.'

'Sorry.'

'Are you sure she'd be able to get a scholarship?' Olly asks Mr Brompton. 'She's got what you might call *natural* intelligence. She's very clever of course,' she rushes to add, as I clench my jaw, 'but she's never been very academically inclined.'

'Dorothy Outhwaite's contributions have been *very much appreciated* over the years.'

'I don't get why this isn't my decision,' I grumble. 'You guys made me come here. At least I can pick my own school.'

'Of course it's your decision, within reason,' snaps Olly. 'I'm just trying to understand. I would never have dreamed you'd want to go to an all-girls school and study robotics. What about your violin?'

Sibbi has slipped into the kitchen. She says, 'Else hasn't got a violin anymore. I'm hungry for jam.'

'What do you mean, Else hasn't got a violin?'

'Shut up, Sibbi,' I say.

Mr Brompton flinches.

'Oh, Else! You didn't leave it on the plane, did you? I'll have to call the airline.'

'Did you see me with it on the plane?' I challenge her.

Olly frowns, trying to remember. 'Did you have it in Hong Kong?'

'You didn't even notice!'

'I had my hands full!' Olly protests.

Dave puts his hands up. 'Everybody slow down. What's going on? Else? Where is it?'

'I left it in Melbourne. In the van.'

'Oh Else, you idiot,' Dave says. He huffs out a sigh. 'I'll call Rick. I don't even know how you post a violin.'

'You don't have to call him. I don't want you to.'

'If I don't call him, then I don't see how we're going to get it back.'

'I don't want it. I left it behind on purpose. I knew you would never understand.'

Mr Brompton clears his throat and stands up. 'Well. I'll just leave you with the paperwork then. I can arrange tours for you, if you'd like some time to decide? No need to see me out, I know the way.'

'No jam,' Sibbi says sadly, and leaves the room before the shouting begins.

CLANCY

ON THE PLANE, I read that the best cure for jetlag is Vitamin D, which comes from sunlight. The only way into the back yard is through the kitchen where the fight between Else and Mum and Dad is building to a noisy crescendo. I let myself quietly out the front door.

The sun is bright and the day is warm. It's a luxury to be warm. Frosty mornings, grey skies, and chilly nights of home feel far, far away. *Home.* The word has never been so foreign.

I sit on the low front wall. London moves around me. Double-decker buses and black taxi cabs navigate the narrow road. Pedestrians walk past with shopping bags. A small child runs ahead of his parents, a dog lags behind on his leash, determinedly sniffing every post, every crack, every stone in the wall.

I wonder if I will ever know this place like I know the hills and creek and wild bushlands at home in Australia. I would like to be a dog, sniffing a map of smells. I close my eyes and takes a deep breath in through my nose. I smell traffic and the river, and history, and people living. An almost-too-sweet, human, *made* kind of smell, like fabric softener. It doesn't smell like Australia at all, but it's not unpleasant.

I open my eyes and see on the wall beside me an enormous brown beetle with large serrated jaws. A stag beetle! I've seen them on David Attenborough. I lean in for a closer look. Being still tired and jetlagged is making the whole world oddly crisp, and I have a sudden impression that the prehistoric-looking stag beetle is very, very big and I am very, very small. I feel a wave of dizziness. I put my hand on the wall to steady myself.

'Don't hurt it. They're endangered. And besides, they don't bite humans.'

'I know!' I say, looking around to see where the voice is coming from. 'I'd *never* hurt a living creature.'

There's a girl in the front garden of the house next door. She looks my age. Her long thick hair and skin and eyes are all dark brown. She's wearing a green singlet dress with an orange T-shirt underneath. She has long green socks, a green silk scarf in her hair, and dangly silver earrings which catch the sunlight.

'My name's Pippa. Do you live here now? My best friend used to live here, but then she went away and died.'

I frown. As far as I know, the only person who lived here was Great-Aunt Dorothy.

Pippa keeps going. 'She was old. She was an old, old lady, but I liked her best of anyone.' Pippa looks at me as if she is deciding something. 'I like you too,' she says in a deciding sort of way. 'I'd never hurt a living creature either.'

I can't help but like Pippa. Was this the way you made a friend? I never knew it could be this easy. Her straight way of talking was so different from the girls on the bus, with their double meanings and confusing facial expressions, where a smile meant the opposite.

'Dorothy was my great-aunt,' I say. 'But I never met her.'

'You'd have liked her.'

I feel sad at the lost opportunity of Great-Aunt Dorothy. It hadn't really occurred to me to wonder what she was like.

'You have an accent,' Pippa says.

I find this surprising, because to me, Pippa is the one with the accent, like she's chewing her words.

'Are you Australian?' she asks.

'Yeah.'

Pippa stares a moment more, and then says, quite loudly, in a peculiar nasal voice, 'Stone the flaming crows!'

'What?'

'That's what that man says.'

I shake my head, mystified.

'On TV.'

'Oh. I don't watch much TV. Mostly David Attenborough documentaries.'

Pippa thinks about this. 'I think if God could talk he'd sound like David Attenborough.'

I find the idea of a giant David Attenborough in the sky incredibly reassuring.

'Don't Australians really talk like that?'

I shake my head.

'Oh,' says Pippa. 'I suppose you can't believe everything you see on television.'

We look at the stag beetle for a while.

'They live under the ground for years,' says Pippa. 'Blind white naked grubs. And then they grow all the proper legs and armour and stuff, and come out into the air for two or three weeks, look for mates, lay their eggs and die. Your aunt left old stumps in the garden and piles of leaves for them to lay their eggs in, which is why you still get a few around here. You won't dig up the stumps, will you?'

'Of course not,' I say. 'You know a lot about them.'

Pippa shrugs. 'Your aunt taught me. She knew a lot about all sorts of things.'

Again I feel a strange tug, like an invisible string connects me to Great-Aunt Dorothy, and Pippa has hold of it. I have never wondered about my love of animals. It comes so naturally to me that it would be like wondering why I have arms or ears. But now it seems it means I belong . . . to Aunt Dorothy, even to England in some way.

'I'd love to go to Australia,' Pippa says. 'I've read so much about it. So much history there. Did you know Australian Aboriginal people are the world's oldest living continuous culture? I mean, that's amazing.'

'Yeah.'

'Do you have any Aboriginal friends in Australia?'

Most of my friends were of the four-legged variety, but wouldn't that sound a bit pathetic? But then I think, if Great-Aunt Dorothy was Pippa's best friend, then Aunty May would count as my friend too. 'My friend Aunty May is Wurundjeri on her dad's side. She mostly grew up with her Dutch mum and her stepdad and his kids, who were all white. She didn't get to know her dad's family until she was a teenager.'

'I'm Jamaican on my mum's side. Mum's grandparents came to England in the nineteen-fifties. But my dad's family is from Scotland and Wales and most of the time I live with him. Mum's got a new boyfriend who doesn't like kids. So I guess I'm sort of like Aunty May.'

'Oh.'

'Families are complicated. Stag beetles make more sense if you ask me.'

Is my family complicated? I've never thought so before, except when Mum has to make two lasagnes – veggie and meat. But then Great-Aunt Dorothy turned up, and that *felt* complicated. There's Nan and Pop, and they don't like Dad much, so that's pretty complicated, for Mum mostly, especially at Christmas. And then there's Aunty May, who isn't our flesh-and-blood family, but feels more like family than Great-Aunt Dorothy or Nan and Pop.

'What's she like? Aunty May?'

'She's like . . . I don't know.' It had never occurred to me to wonder what Aunty May is *like*. She's just Aunty May. 'She taught me how to look after injured native animals. She used to be a park ranger, before she got too old, and she was still the volunteer in our area for injured wildlife. I had to leave Hester behind when we moved here. Hester is a ringtail possum.'

'I wish you could have brought her with you.'

'Hester was ready to look after herself.'

I wonder if Hester misses me, though I know – Aunty May taught me – that animals feelings aren't like human feelings, that they belong to nature, not to people. Being too sentimental about native animals, spoiling them like pets, is as bad as mistreating them.

'Aunty May's in hospital now. Mum says she might not ever go home again.'

'That's what happened to Dorothy.' Pippa stands up and brushes wall dust off herself. 'Want to come and meet my dad? He's making crumpets from a Jamie Oliver recipe. Bespoke crumpets, he calls them. They'll either be nice, or they'll be hideous. Once he made flapjacks that could bounce.'

'Sure,' I say. I'm starving. Definitely dinnertime, I think, following Pippa into the house next door, forgetting all about Hester and Aunty May for now.

ELSE

I STORM UP to the bedroom, haul clothes out of my backpack, pull on my favourite jeans and a clean tank top and my cotton unicorn print cardigan, and step into my sandals. I angrily drag a brush through my hair, pile my hair on top of my head and jab some pins in to hold it in place.

(I mean, I might be angry, but it *is* London.)

'Where are you going, Else?' Sibbi asks.

'Out.'

'Can I come?'

'*No.*'

Sibbi's eyes widen, and her lip begins to tremble.

'Don't you dare start crying,' I hiss at her. 'What have you got to cry about? No one expects anything of you because you're the baby. You stay home and play with Mum or Dad while the rest of us do real work.'

'Playing is real,' Sibbi says. 'Playing *is* my work.'

'Not for long,' I say. I hate myself for being so mean, but I can't help adding, 'Boy, are you in for a surprise.'

ALMOST ANNIE
AND HARDLY ALICE

ALMOST ANNIE WATCHES from the doorway. Hardly Alice is sitting on Else's bed, leaning back on the pillows.

'This is terrible,' Almost Annie whispers.

'This is marvellous!' says Hardly Alice. 'Nothing this interesting has happened in years.'

Almost Annie flickers, worried. She glances upwards. Lately she has felt it more vividly, the dark dreaming of the house, the murmuring of its shadow-self, up in the attic. It wants to be forgotten, and remembered. It wants to be lost, and found. It wants to rage. It wants to be loved. It wants, with such energy, that it's wanting sometimes rattles the bones of the house. But then it forgets itself again, and Annie remembers and forgets too.

ELSE

I TURN RIGHT and start walking. The street is curved and not very wide, but it seems to be a fairly main road with constant traffic. I follow it around and come to a sort of shopping strip, big brand stores (some familiar from home, like The Body Shop and Nine West, some unfamiliar and British-sounding, like Marks & Spencer, Sainsbury's, Boots). Interspersed amongst these are smaller boutique stores and an organic grocer.

I add up and subtract the days we've spent travelling, allowing for stopovers, and work out that it's Saturday morning. The street is alive with shoppers. It all looks like a scene from the Shirley Hughes picture books that Olly read me when I was little and that I then read to the twins and Sibbi, *Dogger* or *Alfie Gets in First*. Two little girls in ballet practice outfits skim the pavement in their ballet slippers, a few boys (and some girls) in footy gear – or soccer, I suppose – weave between slow adults. There are old people shuffling along together with little dogs on leads, and there are young-and-in-love couples.

There's a group of teenage girls my age, wearing similar but somehow different clothes to back home, with similar but somehow different expressions on their faces. Feeling suddenly conspicuous and wrong, I turn away from them, and find myself walking into a churchyard where a jumble sale is being held.

I line up for a coffee. I get to the front of the queue and give my name for the order and then realise I have no English money, just a few Australian gold coins tucked in the pocket of my jeans. Embarrassed, I cancel my mocha, aware that I sound harshly Australian among all the musical English dialects around her.

The churchyard is quite small, but I can't remember where I came in and I start to feel trapped and panicky. I find another exit, by some children's play equipment, but if I walk out that way, I won't be able to retrace my steps home.

Let's take a recap: massive fight with the olds this morning, absolutely hammered by jetlag, and did I really say I wanted to go to some posh girls school? And last but not least, now I'm lost in a foreign country. With no money.

'Um, hello . . . Else?' a voice says. 'You looked like you need this.'

It's a girl – or is a boy? No, a girl, a little younger than me maybe. She's got dyed red hair that points upwards, deliberately or not, I can't tell. I realise she's holding out a takeaway cup with *Else* scrawled on the side.

'Oh,' I say. 'I can't.'

'Of course you can,' the girl says. 'Here –' She takes a sip. 'See? Not poisoned, I promise.'

'Though to be fair, it now has your germs in it,' I say, but it doesn't come out sounding as friendly as I intended.

'Sorry! I'm an idiot. You don't have to drink it, but I'm probably not infectious.'

'It's fine. It was a dumb joke.' I take the cup. 'See. Mm.' I sip it. For some reason I expect British coffee to taste awful, but it's actually okay. Comforting. 'Aren't you having one?'

'I have to go and play.'

'Play?' At first I think she means on the playground, the swings and slides and everything.

'Oh, not that sort of play. Music.'

'Let me guess,' I say, wearily. 'You play the violin.'

'Wow, that is eerie. Are you psychic?'

'More sort of . . . cursed.'

'My name's Adelaide. I play with my friend Ren over there. He's Malaysian, but he grew up in Darwin.'

I look over at a boy with long, straight hair almost to his shoulders, and a long serious face. He's tuning a violin. I turn back to Adelaide, who seems to be waiting for me to say something.

'I don't, like, know him or anything,' I say. 'I've never even been to Darwin.'

'But you *are* from Australia?'

'I flew in from Melbourne yesterday.'

'Oh, wow, intense. How long for?'

I shrug. 'Forever, I guess.'

'Gosh. Well, we play here every fortnight.'

'You better go. It looks like he's waiting for you.'

Adelaide walks over. Ren beats out a staccato rhythm – *Da! da-da-da-dum da-da-da-dum* – that's oddly familiar. It's only when Adelaide starts some long bowing that I realise they're playing the *Doctor Who* theme. I almost laugh. It's pretty cute. They're a sweet couple. Unexpectedly, tears well up in my eyes. It's the jetlag, I tell myself. I take a big gulp of coffee and catch sight of a gap between stalls on the other side of the market, which *might* be where I came in.

More by luck than good management, I find myself back at Outhwaite House. And for once it's not me who is in trouble, but Clancy, who made friends with the next-door neighbour and then disappeared over to her house without telling anyone where he was going. The twins have been off somewhere too, cooking up some scheme, or having some small adventure, unknown to the rest of us as usual.

'We're not at home anymore,' Olly is shouting as I walk in. 'You're all used to a lot of freedom, coming and going when you please. But this is a big city! A foreign country! You can't just wander off without telling us where you're going. And Sibbi, you need to say in the house or the garden – the back garden, not the front.'

'Oh, well –' Dave starts, but Olly flashes him a look, and his words are left hanging in the air. I'm surprised too. It isn't like Olly to be so protective.

'Not the front,' Olly repeats. 'There's traffic, strangers . . . it's a whole country of strangers. You could easily get lost or hurt or – or *worse!* And Oscar, Finn, Clancy, even you, Else. You all need to tell us exactly where you're going and what time you'll be back.'

'Me?' I say. 'Not *me*.'

'We're not in Kansas anymore, Toto,' Finn says.

'We get it,' Oscar adds.

'I really hope you do,' says Olly, and she glares at me. 'Life has changed for the Outhwaite family. We all need to get used to it.'

In my room, I open up my laptop and send Sam an email.

I left my violin in the van in Australia. Am I the most ridiculous human in the history of the universe?

I wait, but it must be the middle of the night there or something, because Sam doesn't respond.

CLANCY

'MR BROMPTON HAS organised the school tours,' Dad says at dinner.

'Already?' Else says.

'We've been here a week,' says Dave.

Only a week? It's starting to feel normal to me. I've had the odd twinge of homesickness, but England is just *there*, all the time, out the window, out the front door. And Pippa is there too, when she isn't at school.

Mum dishes up bowls of tomato soup. I tear open a seedy roll and reach for the butter and cheese.

Else rolls her eyes. 'We don't *need* to go on a tour. We've got the brochures.'

'You'll have to take the children,' Mum says to Dad. 'I promised my supervisor I'd get a chapter of my thesis to her this week and it's a mess.'

Dad frowns. 'I suppose I can make that work. I might have to push back the meeting with the estate lawyers. You sure you don't want to come and look over the schools too? I thought you would be interested.'

Mum hesitates a moment. But she shakes her head, *no*.

Mum has hardly left Outhwaite House since we arrived. She resists all invitations to walk down to the banks of the Thames or go to Richmond Park to see the hipster deer. We haven't been to a single museum or art gallery or historic building or any of the other touristy things Dad brings home brochures for. She's always muttering about *deadlines* and *milestones*, promising to take us *tomorrow, next week. Soon. Sometime. Not now. Later. Soon.*

ALMOST ANNIE
AND HARDLY ALICE

'DOROTHY WAS MISERABLE at that school,' Almost Annie frets, as Else stands at the hallway mirror, dragging her fingers through her knotty hair. Of course Else can't see or hear Almost Annie, but she scowls anyway.

'Was she?' asks Hardly Alice, distractedly. She and Sibbi are both hunched over Oscar in the living room, watching him play a game on Dave's phone.

'Oh, you and your memory!' says Annie. 'The only the reason she donated so much money was to try to prevent girls being as miserable as she was. She practically built the science wing herself. Though I'd have gone with a library myself.' Alive, Annie was not a proficient reader – her education cut short when she was sent out to work – but death has given her plenty of time to refine the art, sitting beside Dorothy, reading over her shoulder.

'Mm?' Alice says, craning her neck to see Oscar's screen better. 'I'd have liked to be a scientist. Or an engineer. I'd like to know how these things work.'

'Well, you'd have been a century and a half too early, at least.'

'What do you think stopped us from inventing these things, in our day?'

Almost Annie shakes her head in disbelief. '*Our* day? You're fifty years older than I am. At least!'

'Am I?' Hardly Alice asks, distracted. 'Oh, honestly, child! Tilt left, not right! If only *I* could drive it.'

Hardly Alice loses patience with Oscar and wanders over to stand beside Else, who is at the mirror, fiddling nervously with her hair. Of course Else can't see Alice's image reflected in the glass, but Alice sees herself. Her hand rises to her own hair, always perfectly done up on top of her head. 'I feel *this* is my day, really. Change happens all the time, but at such a glacial pace, that it is as if nothing really changes at all. Don't you think? Summer, winter, dinner, breakfast, all of them different, and yet all of them the same.'

'Oh, everything changes. So many changes! People change. They come and go. Children grow up so fast. Once it was Miss Dorothy and her brothers, rest their souls, and now we have Miss Sibbi and Master Oscar and Master Finn and . . .'

'Much of a muchness though, aren't they? I mean they could all have been here before. A brother, a cousin, a nephew, an uncle, a baby, a very old man. One into the other. Copies. Repeats.'

'All so very different, though,' Almost Annie protests.

'And yet,' Hardly Alice repeats, studying her own face next to Else's, 'all very much the same.'

ELSE

As we walk down the hallways of Kingsley College, the achingly familiar sound of tuning instruments drifts out of the practice rooms and I almost can't bear it. Even I can see it's a nice school, close to the river, in a leafy street, though the grounds are flat and treeless, with large expanses of soft-fall and spongy green lawns. The buildings are modern and geometrically interesting, with lots of space and light in the classrooms. The girls and boys wear the same grey shorts; the V-neck jumpers are a cheerful shade of blue.

'It's great,' says Dave. 'So well resourced compared to your old school, don't you think, Else?'

I don't answer.

'It smells funny,' says Sibbi.

Mr Nhill, the headteacher, doesn't bat an eyelid. 'A select group of our musicians are invited to workshops at the Royal Academy of Music throughout the year. Your dad tells me you're a keen violinist, Else. Have you got Royal Academy aspirations?'

I shrug. 'I'm not *that* keen.'

'She's having a bit of a hiatus,' Dave says, shooting me a death look. 'With the move and all.'

'I hope you're practising every day,' Mr Nhill says. 'You don't want to fall behind. What about you boys? Do you play anything?'

Oscar says, 'Apparently we could only afford one musical genius in the family.'

'Oscar!' Dave is mortified. Even I'm embarrassed by the way we are all behaving. I will myself to ask something about the music programme, but I can't think of a single thing to say.

'Oh, hello there!' A passing student stops in her tracks. I recognise her strangely upwards-sweeping hair. 'You're Australian and I'm Adelaide, remember? We met the other day. At the farmer's market? I gave you my germs?'

I don't want to be rude, but I don't want Dave to think I've been off happily making friends like Clancy, especially not a friend who goes to this school, and definitely not a violin-playing friend.

'G'day,' says Dave. 'I'm Else's dad. What do *you* think of the school?'

'Oh, you know, it's school.' Adelaide makes a face and then meets Mr Nhill's gaze. 'Ahem. Which is to say I love it. Love. It. Well-rounded education. Top-notch teachers.'

When Adelaide is gone, Mr Nhill says, 'Very talented violinist.'

'Technically proficient, I suppose,' I say, and feel mean, though it is true that Adelaide played the *notes* well, while Ren played with more feeling, but less technique.

96

'Exceptionally technically proficient,' sniffs Mr Nhill.

I think of Sam's return email, that I just received this morning. *You are definitely the most ridiculous human in the world,* he'd written back. *What are you going to do without your violin?*

'What do you teach?' asks Dave.

'I run the music program,' says Mr Nhill.

Mr Nhill hates us.

The twins seem happy enough with Kingsley. There's enough sport to keep Oscar happy and if Oscar is happy, Finn is happy. Or happy enough. Clancy's happy because he'll be back at the same school as the twins since the way their birthdays fall they'll be able to start high school six months earlier than in Australia. Besides, this is where Pippa goes.

'Am I going here?' says Sibbi.

'No,' says Dave.'

And then Sibbi is happy too.

SIBBI

WE ALL CATCH a bus back up Mortlake Road, towards Lady Emily Hartington and Penrose Infant School.

'I suppose it's convenient that they're close together,' says Daddy. 'You could take Sibbi on the bus, Else.'

'On the bus to where? There's our house,' says Sibbi.

The boys ring the bell and the bus stops right outside Outhwaite House.

Sibbi waves up to the top windows. 'Hello, naughty house.'

'Why naughty?' says Daddy.

'It thinks in bad words,' says Sibbi. 'It hates itself.'

'Oh,' says Daddy. 'I don't like the word *hate*.'

'I told you it was naughty.'

'It's just a word,' says Else. 'Like any other word. Why are some words good and some words bad? It's *stupid*.'

'That sort of radical thinking might not go down too well at Ladypants High.'

'*Stupid* is a bad word too,' says Sibbi.

But Daddy and Else are lost in an argument of their own.

'Why do you keep making comments like that?' Else snaps. 'What's wrong with a girls school anyway? I'm a girl. *Sibbi's* a girl. Other parents would be glad I want to broaden my horizons.'

'Sure, but broaden your horizons at Kingsley. Take science. Join the chess club. But keep your options open. Don't give up something you've worked at . . .'

'What about you? You gave up being a lawyer to build fences. Nan and Pop thought *that* was crazy.'

'That was different. I was never passionate about being a lawyer.'

'But you didn't like building fences either.'

Daddy shrugs. 'I guess I'm still working out what I want to be when I grow up.'

'But you *are* grown up, Daddy,' Sibbi says.

'So are you a lawyer again now?' Else says.

'I'm helping Mr Brompton and he's paying me enough to tide us over while we wait for the estate to settle.'

'And then what?'

Sibbi looks at Daddy and Daddy looks out the window. 'I don't know,' he says quietly to Else. 'Right now I'm just dealing with one thing at a time.'

ELSE

I'M NOT SURE what I'm expecting – Hogwarts perhaps – but in the end Lady Emily Hartington is just a school. Very clean, much cleaner than my old school. Nice white tiled halls, shiny science labs. Sparkling windows. But it still smells like any old school: pencil shavings and floor cleaner.

Anyway, it's *fine*. The girls are all nice and boring in that way that people you don't know always are. Some look catty, some look gloomy, some look kind, and that would be the same at any school. I'd thought because of the fancy uniforms and the money they'd all be different but somewhere in the school there's probably a Kasey and an Audrey and a Tilly and a Camille, or girls just like them, one just like me even.

Ivy, the head girl, takes us around the school on a lightning-fast tour, flinging her arm in the direction of toilets and maths classrooms and food labs. She is brisk and long-faced, like an English girl from a TV show or a member of the royal family, like she's playing the character of herself and she's not a real person at all, and she doesn't seem the least bit interested in us, despite my fascinating, fresh from *Neighbours* accent. Oddly Sibbi takes a liking to her, and holds her hand all around the school, clinging on a bit too long at the end, which is embarrassing for everyone, especially Ivy who has to prise herself free. Embarrassing for everyone, except for Sibbi who cries real angry tears and shows no shame.

SIBBI

Sibbi's school is a three-storey building, dark and grim. Sibbi is not interested in the classrooms. Else and Daddy look silently at the tiny children sitting at desks, cutting pre-printed shapes out with scissors.

'Does Sibbi even know how to use scissors?' Daddy whispers to Else and she shrugs.

Sibbi shrinks away from the large lunch room, and even Else feels an unbearable loneliness enter her as she looks at the light streaming in the imposing arched windows, breathing in the almost suffocating smell of roast meat and jacket potatoes.

'Are the children *happy* at school?' Else asks Mrs Butterworth, the head teacher.

'Oh yes,' says Mrs Butterworth.

'All of them?' asks Else.

'Very happy,' says Mrs Butterworth, firmly.

'Aren't there any other schools?' Else asks Daddy as they walk out the grim school gate. She pictures the playground at the old primary school they left behind. The big green oval, the monkey bars, the long slide, the gazebo, the netball courts, the permaculture garden, the fruit trees espaliered on the wire fence, the kookaburras, the lizards, and all the funny dips and crevasses and hiding places.

Daddy doesn't like it much either. 'What choice do we have?' he says to Else. 'We were lucky to get a spot here. And she has to go *somewhere*. It's the law.'

Sibbi says nothing. She leans against Dave, bumping gently against him. The bus rocks from side to side, rocking her to sleep.

CLANCY

'HAVE YOU NOTICED that Mum never wants to go anywhere?' I ask Else, who's reading in the lounge room.

Else shrugs. 'She's busy writing her thesis.'

'We've come all the way across the world, and we haven't seen *anything*. Big Ben. Buckingham Palace. The Imperial War Museum. The British Library.'

Else turns the page of her book, but I bet if she's honest with herself, she can't remember what she's read for the last ten pages. 'You could go. You just have to catch the Tube. You could work it out by yourself.'

'But you heard Mum. She's not going to let us go wandering around England by ourselves. But she'd let me go if you came with me.'

'All right,' Else says. 'Where would we go?'

'The Natural History Museum,' I say, not missing a beat.

Else flops back down. 'No way. Go with Pippa.'

'She's been a million times. I want to go with you. I want to go today. Look.' I show her the tourist map. 'It's right next to the Victoria & Albert Museum. And see, there's the Albert Hall.'

Else studies the map. I watch her finger land on the map, a few blocks from the Museum of Natural History. I read over her shoulder: *The Royal Academy of Music.*

'All right. You tell Mum.'

But when I go and tell Mum, Sibbi says, 'I go too?'

I look at Mum.

'Just Clancy and Else this time, love.'

'No-oo!' Since we moved to London, Sibbi has no orange light, I've noticed. She flips straight from green to red with no warning. She roars. 'NO! No go-oo.'

Else comes in. 'Oh, not again, Sibbi.'

Mum looks at Else. 'Can't you take Sibbi with you?'

'No way,' says Else.

'Where are the twins?' I ask.

'Playing soccer at the park,' Mum says.

'Where's Dad?' says Else.

'At Mr Brompton's office.'

'Again?' I say.

'Mr Brompton's letting us save some money by sorting through the estate ourselves. It's all in a bit of a mess. Dad's got some experience with contract law from before Sibbi was born, but he's not that familiar with the law in England.'

'Save money? I don't understand. If we've inherited this house . . .?'

'It's complicated. All the money's tied up in *things* – the house, silverware, even the furniture. With taxes and the financial crisis and chasing paperwork around, we're not even sure exactly what we've inherited yet. It's hard to know what has value and what's just rubbish.'

I shudder. 'Ugh. Money, money, money. If this is what it's like to be rich, I think I'd rather be poor.'

'Can't Sibbi go with you?' Mum pleads. 'I really need to get some writing done today.'

'No,' says Else. 'She's hard work. She'll run off, she doesn't listen. It's not like Australia, people don't want to put up with ratty kids here.'

'I want to go on the Tube train,' Sibbi gulps between sobs. 'I want to go the museum. I want to go to Buckingham Palace. I want to see a queen . . . and a pussycat . . . and a Baby Prince George.'

'We're not going to Buckingham Palace anyway,' says Else.

'Sibbi, you stay here and be Mummy's big helper,' I say.

'No! No big helper!'

'Why don't we all go?' I say to Mum. 'You come too. You can have one day off working, can't you?'

But Mum takes gentle hold of Sibbi's arms. 'Just go. Have you got enough money? Do you have a map? Are you sure you're going to be okay? Go, then. Go quickly. Be back by three. *Ouch!* Sibbi! You *bit* me!'

'Sibbi!' I can't believe it. Sibbi has never *bitten* anyone. 'Are you okay, Mum?'

'Just go!'

Sibbi throws herself at us – even as the door is closing in her face – and screams. Mum struggles to hold her back.

'I feel awful,' I say to Else.

'I don't,' says Else. 'I feel nothing.'

ELSE

THE TUBE IS surprisingly easy to figure out – we get off at South Kensington, climb up to street level, and then we are right there. There's a queue to get in; we join the queue. I notice that most of the families come in sets of twos: two parents, two kids. Language weaves around us, not everyone is speaking English.

Clancy nudges her, 'Listen, they're Australian.'

Three girls, a few years older than me, are ahead of us in the queue. There's a slow, easy way that they make their vowels and a huskiness to their voices that makes me suddenly, sharply homesick. I tune in instead to the family behind us, a girl in a headscarf trying to keep her younger siblings in the queue while her parents chat between themselves. I don't need to understand the language to know what the older girl is saying.

The queue moves quickly. We get inside and realise we don't need to pay anyone, though there are donation bins.

'How much should we give?' Clancy whispers. I understand his urge to whisper – the massive entrance with its grand staircases and vaulted ceilings, feels holy, like a church.

I reach into my pocket and pull out a few gold coins. The pounds look like Australian two-dollar coins – confusing. The two-pound coins are bigger, gold encircling a silver centre. I give one to Clancy and drop one in myself.

We wander through the exhibits.

'Look.' I draw Clancy's attention to a picture of a woman called Mary Anning. 'She discovered a whole dinosaur skeleton at the beach when she was eleven. What have you been doing with your life?'

'Too late for me now,' says Clancy.

'We've wasted our youth,' I agree. 'Oh look!' I say, turning a corner. 'Dodos! Real live dead dodos!'

Clancy gazes silently at the dodos. We wander past the birds, including some familiar friends from home, all stuffed and arranged in the glass cases, telling the story, not just of the bird world, but of the human history of empire and expansion. We walk through to another gallery. I study the tiny skull of a Neanderthal baby. *It was alive once*, I say to myself, experimentally, trying to conjure up feeling, but I can't make myself believe it. I'm starting to wonder if I'm emotionally dead inside.

SIBBI

THEY ARE FORGETTING me, Sibbi says to the mirror's lonely eyes. *They are always forgetting me.*

In the attic, something is waking. Waking more every day, feeding on all that energy, all that chaos, the dark swirling dust devil of Sibbi's resentment and sorrow and loneliness. It sends out its own cold, damp shadow made of years of abandonment and neglect, a cloud that drifts through the house and into Sibbi's heart. When Sibbi looks at herself in the mirror, she sees its loneliness reflected back at her. She thinks it is her own loneliness she is seeing.

Sibbi goes into Great-Aunt Dorothy's study, even though Daddy told her not to. The room is lined with bookshelves with double layers of books, and then more books higgledy-piggledy, sideways, wedged in wherever they will fit. There are boxes and boxes of paper.

Sibbi opens the top drawer of the desk. In the drawer are lots of intriguing bits and pieces. Typewriter ribbons and a plastic container with a magnetic lid to which paperclips cling. There's a box of ivory cards, an envelope filled with rubber bands of assorted colours and sizes, a stapler and a thick black permanent marker. She touches the permanent marker, it's stubby thickness promising to destroy or create, but her hand keeps moving. She might come back for the permanent marker, but for now she chooses the big scissors.

She picks them up. They have heft to them. They are glitteringly sharp, proper grown-up scissors that will cut through anything.

She isn't ready to use them. She doesn't know what they are for. Not yet. She takes them back to her bedroom and hides them under the bed. For scissors are useful things, and all useful things have a purpose, if you wait and you listen and you see.

CLANCY

'Let's go,' I say.

'You want to skip the rest of Human Evolution?' Else asks.

I shake his head vigorously. 'I want to leave.'

'Leave? We've just got here. You know we'll have to queue to get back in?'

'I don't want to get back in.'

Else shakes her head, mystified. 'Okay. Let's go.' I follow her to an exit. 'Was it the human skulls? I thought you liked nature.'

'Nature? I *love* nature. But this is not a museum about nature! It's a museum about humans ripping nature off. A museum of taking what doesn't belong to you, just because, just to have. They aren't even animals anymore, they're just . . . objects. Ugh.'

'But what were you expecting? You knew everything in here would be dead, right?'

I shake my head. 'I don't know.'

'It's raining again,' Else says.

I'm slowly getting used to the grey drizzle that comes and goes most days. Every day the forecast is the same: sunshine and showers. Sunshine and showers.

'Did you know,' Else says, 'that the Royal Academy of Music is just up that road?'

'Let's go and look! Aren't you curious?'

Else grimaces. But I take off, knowing she'll follow. She's hardly going to leave me stranded in a London borough all on my own. 'Come on. At least see what you're missing out on.'

'Let's go back to the Tube station,' Else says, a bit further up the road. 'Let's go and get a drink. I'm thirsty.'

'You must be a little bit interested or you wouldn't have told me it was here.'

'I wish I'd never said anything. I don't even have a violin anymore, remember? I couldn't play even if I wanted to.'

'Aha!'

'Aha, what?'

'Even if you *wanted to*.'

'But I *don't* want to.'

'Then why do you want to go and look at the Royal Academy?'

'I *don't*.'

'Well, then why do you *not* want to look at the Royal Academy? If you didn't care, you'd just look at it anyway, wouldn't you?'

'Oh, stop trying to be so clever.'

'Wait, is this it?'

We stand and stare up at the sculpture, great stone men staring out, and hunched beneath them, figures of men and women, bent towards the earth, looking like they're calling something up.

'Not music though,' says Else. 'Look, it's the Royal School of *Mines*.'

'Huh. Engineering, I suppose. The Music Academy must be a bit further up.'

'I've seen enough,' says Else. 'I don't want to see any more.'

'But we're nearly there.'

Else turns on her heel and marches off. I wait for a moment to see if she'll come back for me, but she doesn't.

'Wait for me!' I shout, but she doesn't wait, and I have to run to keep up or be lost in London on my own.

ELSE

I COMPOSE EMAILS to Sam in my head, but I never get around to writing them down and sending them. Days pass and there never seems to be anything important enough to say. I sleep late into the morning. I snap at Sibbi, avoid the twins and Clancy and Pippa, pointedly ignore Olly and rarely see Dave. I wait until the house is quiet before I go downstairs. In a grudging concession towards Olly's newfound paranoia, I leave vague scrawled notes: *Going out. Back later.* And then I just wander. Up Mortlake Road to High Street, sometimes down to the riverbank. But I prefer crowds. I like wandering the supermarket and looking at the weird food, or browsing stores like Top Shop and Marks & Spencer, though I don't buy anything. I test the samples at Boots. I tell myself that I'm mysterious, interesting, aloof. I watch myself walking up the street, as though I am Audience to my life rather than Actor.

Today Ren is playing solo outside the organic grocery store. I linger, watching him from across the street, his eyes half closed, listening intently to his own music. Ren is not the least bit interested in me, probably wouldn't know me from a bar of soap, which gives me space to be interested in him. The couple who run the organic grocery shop are Ren's parents. I can tell this because when they bring him cut-up fruit or a cup of tea, he looks annoyed rather than grateful. His playing *is* less technically accomplished than Adelaide's, but his wrists are more relaxed. There's a fluid pleasure in his playing and I enjoy listening to it.

Ren's music follows people walking down the street. A group of children run past him, and his violin catches their happy shouts and tosses them wildly into the air. A mother tells off her small child. The violin scrapes, *Why?* and then a few quick notes reply: *Because I said so.* An elderly couple walks past, arm in arm. The violin begins a Victorian waltz, and the couple's feet seem to keep the time.

'Do you play?' I turn to see Adelaide at my side. Damn. Sprung.

'No. Why do you ask?' I realise I am holding my hands as if I am holding an invisible violin. I drop my arms guiltily to my sides, then I resent Adelaide for making me feel guilty.

'What do you think of Ren's playing?'

'It's a nice violin. Big sound.'

Adelaide beams. 'It's brilliant! My grandfather made it.'

'Made it? What do you mean?'

'My grandad is a world-famous violin maker. He gave one to Princess Kate and Prince William for George when he was a baby.'

'Couldn't they afford to buy him one?'

'It's a big deal, actually. It was in all the major papers, and it's going on a tour of the world soon. Grandad's very well respected.'

'Cool,' I say, flatly, though it does sound pretty interesting.

'You can meet him if you're interested. Grandad, I mean, not Prince George. He's just around the corner.'

Adelaide's face is open and kind, as if she doesn't ever notice how badly I behave, how rude and reticent I am.

I cannot seem to help my rudeness, this invisible barrier between me and the rest of the world. Even at the dinner table, surrounded by her family, I am imprisoned in my own mood. At night after everyone else has gone to bed I wander the house, as silent as the ghosts Sibbi keeps claiming to see. I get on the internet and lurk, watching my friends chatting online, but I never have anything to say. I read the emails they send me and look at the photographs. I am a ghost, watching from a great distance, never answering.

'Come on,' says Adelaide. 'It's not far from here.'

And then I'm caught up in her wake, not exactly saying yes, but somehow not saying no either.

ELSE

ADELAIDE KEEPS UP a steady stream of chatter, and perhaps this is what keeps me tethered to her. I don't contribute anything to the conversation. Adelaide seems the type to not take anything personally.

'Here we are,' she says. 'Just down here. Look, you can see the sign.'

Lev Starman
Violin and Bow Maker.
Maintenance, Restoration, Repair.

Adelaide goes down and taps on the door. 'He's not answering,' she calls.

'Oh well.' I turn to go, though I admit I am a tiny bit disappointed.

'Oh no, it's all right,' Adelaide says. 'I've got a key. Grandad won't mind. I'd say he's having a kip upstairs.'

'Kip? Isn't that smoked fish?'

'That's kipper,' Adelaide says. 'And my grandfather is Slovenian. And vegetarian. So he prefers pickled turnips, which are actually surprisingly tasty, especially with cheese.'

I stand on the footpath, watching Adelaide disappear into the shop. Okay, so I could just walk away right now. Why am I here anyway, torturing myself by looking at something I can't have anymore? But wait, I didn't even want my violin anyway. I'd made my own decision, just like I was always saying I should. That's what it meant to be grown up – making a decision and sticking to it. Like Dave should have done with the fences.

Adelaide stuck her head out of the shop. 'So are you coming?'

It wouldn't hurt to just *look*. Just to prove to myself that I can be here, be around violins, and it doesn't matter. And I've never seen a violin being made. It's natural that I'd still be interested in that, even if I didn't want to play myself anymore. I could have a quick look, and then go home.

I expect it to be dark and close in the workshop, so I'm surprised when I step through the low doorway to find sun streaming in through high windows.

All around the walls and on the work benches are parts of violins, bodies without necks, ribs laid out, jars of pegs, tail-guts.

It makes me feel sad for my lost violin. Not sorry for myself, but sorry for the instrument, quiet in its case. I hope Rick will discover it on his travels, and find it a home, maybe with some teenage girl in the middle of nowhere who'll appreciate the gift.

'See.' Adelaide points to an impossibly tiny violin. 'Did you ever have a quarter size, or even an eighth? That's a sixty-fourth.'

Okay. Despite myself, I'm charmed. 'For Prince George? It looks like a toy.'

'It really plays,' says Adelaide.

'Do you think George ever actually played it?'

Adelaide shrugs. 'Grandad's getting it ready to go on tour.'

We hear steps, shuffling overhead.

'That's Grandad,' says Adelaide. 'I'll just go and tell him we're here.'

'Oh no, don't . . . *please* don't.' My heart is racing, though I don't know why. 'I should leave. I didn't mean to bother him.'

'It's no bother. Would you like to play one?'

'No.'

'Go on, I'd love to hear you play. I bet you're brilliant.'

'I'm really not,' I tell her.

'I'll be back in two ticks,' Adelaide says. 'I'll make us a coffee and see if Grandad's about. Stay here.'

In the studio alone with the violins, the temptation to play is strong. Maybe there's no harm in just picking one up, holding it to my shoulder.

There's a full-sized violin sitting in an open case near the door. I pick it up. My muscles ache with remembering. I lift it to my chin. My other arm wants a bow. Potential energy fizzes in the air, like the moment in a performance when the conductor lifts their arms.

'Well, Adelaide's friend. Are you going to play something?'

I jump and turns around.

'I'm sorry,' says the violin-maker. 'I did not mean to startle you.'

He isn't so very old: his eyes and his hands are young. But his curly hair is silver grey and his face is creased from frowning at fine, detailed work.

'There's no bow.' I put the violin gently back in the case.

The violin-maker raises his eyebrows and gazes deliberately around the walls, lined with bows. 'What would you have played?' he asks.

The only piece I can think of is the Mozart. 'I don't play,' I say. 'Not anymore.'

'I see,' says the violin-maker. He looks at me a long time.

'I mean, I used to. But I guess I got as good as I was going to get.'

The violin-maker nods. He picks up a bow from the bench and inspects it, then swaps it for another. He tightens the tension screw and hands it to me with a piece of rosin. Automatically, again more from muscle memory than conscious thought, I rub rosin on the bow.

'I mean,' I say, a little defensively. 'I was pretty good. You know. But there's a point –'

'It stopped being enjoyable. It became work.'

'Yes. Well, no!' I frown, confused. 'I don't mind *work*.'

'Ah,' he says, and thinks for a moment. 'So. There was no flow.'

I'm trying to be annoyed at this quick, brutal assessment of my highly personal, complicated situation. I don't know exactly what he means by this word – *flow* – and yet it is acutely precise. Playing stopped being unconscious and fluid – flowing. I no longer felt like an extension of the instrument. My movements had become jagged and awkward, as if my body and the violin were resisting each other.

Adelaide calls down the stairs, 'Would you like sugar in your coffee, Else?'

'No thanks,' I say. I offer the bow to the violin-maker and he takes it. He picks up the violin I was playing and plays a few bright notes.

He says, 'The world is not waiting for you to play the violin.'

I realise I've been holding my breath. 'Sorry? What?'

'No one will ask you to play. No one will miss you. I have seen great players give up, and no one comes looking for them. There are many other great players to take their place.'

'Sure,' I say. 'I get it. I'm not special.'

'But I think,' the man continues as if I haven't spoken, 'I think you will miss it. I think you are already missing it, and that is why you are here.'

I feel the small room closing in. I look at the empty, half-built violins, the stray parts, and suddenly it looks like a room full of bones. I step back towards the door.

'Tell Adelaide . . . Oh, don't worry. Don't tell her anything. Or tell her sorry. I *am* sorry. I should never have come.'

I fall out the door into the alley, take a breath and runs. I run fast, run until my breath comes out in ragged sobs. I run all the way back to Outhwaite House where I stop, because I have nowhere else to go. I look down and realises I am still holding the violin-maker's rosin in my hand.

SIBBI

'I ARE LONELY,' says Sibbi.

Lo-o-onely, sighs the shadow in the attic.

'Hang on a minute,' says Olly, typing. 'Let me just finish this ...' She looks up. 'Oh, Sibbi, I'm sorry. Give me five minutes, and then I'll come and play with you.'

Sibbi goes into the hallway. She drags her finger along the wall. She goes back into the kitchen. 'Has it been five minutes?' she asks.

'Sibbi,' Olly says. 'No.'

One minute later: 'What about now?'

'Sibbi! The more you pester, the longer I'll take.'

Sibbi goes back into the hallway. Oscar and Finn burst through the open front door and Sibbi glimpses the street, trees and sunlight.

'Hey, Sibmonster!" Finn says. 'What's doing?'

'I'm being lonely,' Sib says. 'I'm always being so alone-ly.'

The front door opens again. A bicycle bell rings. A truck rattles past. Somebody calls to a cat. And then the door closes and the hallway is dim and quiet. It's Clancy and Pippa this time.

Olly comes out into the hallway. 'Oh great, you're all here. You can play with Sib then.' She disappears back into the kitchen.

CLANCY

'CAN'T YOU TAKE her?' Oscar says to me and Pippa. 'We were just going to grab our cricket gear and head back to the park. There's a game starting and they said they'd wait five minutes for us.'

'We played Go Fish with her yesterday,' I say.

Sibbi's wide eyes go from Oscar to me, back to Oscar.

'We could play something else,' Finn says, taking pity on Sibbi. 'What about Kick the Can?'

'The back yard's too small for Kick the Can,' says Oscar. 'There's not enough hiding places.'

'What's Kick the Can?' Pippa asks.

'We can play it inside,' says Finn.

'It's too loud,' I say. 'It'll upset Mum. It's a cross between hide-and-seek, and tiggy,' I tell Pippa. 'Or tag or chasey, whatever you call it here.'

'What about Sardines, then?' Pippa suggests. 'That's a good one for indoors.'

'How do you play?'

Pippa quickly runs through the rules. One person hides and everyone else looks. If they find the hider, they squeeze in and hide too, everyone squished in together like sardines in a tin.

'Shall we do dip-dip?' Oscar says.

We all stick a foot in, including Sibbi.

'There's a party on the hill would you like to come,' chants Oscar.

His finger lands on me.

'Yes,' I say.

'Then bring a bottle of rum-a-tum-tum,' Oscar sings. His finger points to Pippa's foot.

'What do I say?' she asks.

'Can't afford it,' answers Finn.

'Can't afford it,' says Pippa.

'Then pack your bags and off you go.'

Finn pulls his foot in.

'We do it differently,' Pippa says. 'There's a party on the hill, can you come? Say yes.'

'Yes,' says Oscar.

'Bring your own bread and butter and a bun.' Pippa's finger rests on Sibbi. 'It's the same.'

'Can't afford it,' says Sibbi.

'Who is your best friend?' Pippa's finger lands on me this time. She looks at me expectantly.

'You,' I say, and it gives me a strange tickle at the back of my mouth. I've never had a best friend before.

Pippa keeps chanting. 'Pippa will be there with her knickers in the air. O-U-T spells out.'

It goes around a couple more times, until it's between Oscar and Sibbi. 'Hang on a sec,' Oscar says, just as it's about to land on him. 'Let's do it our way.'

'That's cheating,' says Pippa. 'You just don't want to be It.'

'Oh, come on,' says Finn. 'Don't start fighting. Just do it again or we'll never play.'

Of course Sibbi is It. Pippa shoots Oscar a filthy look.

'You hide first,' says Pippa. 'And if we find you, we hide with you. Do you understand how to play?'

'She's not stupid,' says Oscar.

SIBBI

EVERYONE CLOSES THEIR eyes and begins to count together. Sibbi runs up the stairs. She runs right up, up to the third floor where Clancy and the twins and her parents' bedrooms are. She goes to the attic door and jiggles the handle. It's still locked, but it wants to be opened.

The others are coming. Sibbi slips behind her parent's door and waits.

She hears her own breath. She hears the children walking up the stairs and around the second floor.

She hears, very faintly, the rattle of the locked door . . .

She feels something slip in next to her, hide beside her . . .

She reaches out. It's Finn. Her hand finds his and they press in together, waiting for the others.

ALMOST ANNIE
AND HARDLY ALICE

ALMOST ANNIE SIGHS. 'They grow up so fast, don't they?'

'Do you think?' says Hardly Alice. 'I think it takes *forever*.'

'Remember when Pippa could see us? Strange how they grow out of it.'

'*He* sees us sometimes,' Alice says, pointing at Finn. 'He thinks he does anyway. Just out of the corner of his eye, but if he turns around . . . There's nothing there.'

'There is,' says Annie. 'There's us.'

'Yes,' sighs Alice. 'Here we are. Here we always are.'

CLANCY

DOWNSTAIRS, OSCAR SAYS to Pippa, 'Watch out for Sibbi's ghosts.'

'Ghosts?' asks Pippa. 'There are no ghosts. I'd know if there were ghosts here.' She looks only the slightest bit uncertain.

'Are there really ghosts here?' Pippa whispers when Oscar goes looking in the lounge room.

'Only Sibbi's seen them,' I say. 'Though . . .'

'What?'

'Well. There *is* something creepy about that door upstairs, the locked one.'

'You mustn't ever open the upstairs door,' Pippa says, and then puts her hand to her mouth. 'I don't know why I said that. But I know it's true.'

'I know,' I say. 'It's weird. It needs to stay locked. But it wants to be opened.'

'A door can't *want* anything.'

'I know. A *door* can't. So what . . .?'

'Wa-ha-ha-ha-HA!' Oscar leaps out at us from Dorothy's study, then falls about laughing. 'Scaredy cats.'

'Are not,' says Pippa. But we stick close together on the stairs.

ELSE

IT TAKES ME a few days of exploring to find my way back to Lev Starman, Violin-maker. When I finally find the alleyway, I realise I've already walked past it at least once, maybe twice, it's so narrow and hidden away.

I dig the rosin out of my canvas satchel, and knock on the workshop door. I wait. No answer, but perhaps he's upstairs? I knock again. After an age, I hear him shuffle down the stairs.

He opens the door and looks at me uncertainly.

I hold out the rosin. He grunts and steps aside, inviting me in.

'I'm sorry,' I say. 'I didn't meant to take it.'

Lev Starman shrugs. 'I did not even notice it was gone.' He looks around the studio. 'I would hardly notice a violin missing until someone came in asking for it.'

'What are you working on today?' I ask, curious despite myself. 'The little violin for Prince George?'

'A bauble. A toy. What does a small child need with a violin? Likely he will never play it, or even touch it and one day it will end up in a museum somewhere. A quaint curiosity.' He tilts his head and looks at me. 'That's how you feel, isn't it?'

'Why *are* you making it then?'

'No one requires its existence, yet it exists. It amused me to make it, and it hurts no one. And if there is a message in it, it is that music is important, even if you are a little king.'

When I think about music, it makes me feel dizzy, like I'm standing at the edge of a cliff, looking down. Music is so big, much bigger than me. I used to believe in it, it used to fit in the palm of my hand like a secret, or a present. Now I'm not sure what I believe in.

'Look at this one here. This is one of the first violins I ever made. It is the one you were holding the other day, yes?'

I look at the instrument and nod, remembering the weight of it in my hands.

'The woman I made it for died a few years ago. Her husband flew back with it from America to return it to me. The instrument outlived the player. It will outlive its maker too. Isn't that extraordinary?'

But what is the purpose, I wonder, of a violin without a player? Why exist, even forever, if you are never played?

'The little king's violin is finished,' Lev Starman tells me. 'You may take a look if you like. I must go back upstairs now to my paperwork, for the bills don't pay themselves any more than a violin can make itself. You can let yourself out.'

'Are you . . . are you sure? You hardly know me!'

Lev Starman laughs. 'You came back, four days later, to bring me rosin.' He shrugs again. 'I think you are a good girl. Please. Play one, if you want.'

Lev Starman shuffles back up the staircase. I am filled with pity for him for being old. (And yet I suspect that Lev Starman pities me for being young.)

I walk over to the workbench and open the tiny violin case and look at Prince George's tiny violin. I wish I had brought Sibbi with me to see it. I feel a pang of guilt, thinking of Sibbi sitting on the steps at home with her chin resting on her arms, watching me go. I shake my head to get rid of the vision. Lev Starman, Violin-maker, is wrong. I am not sure what I am or who I am meant to be without music. But I am quite sure I am not a good girl.

SIBBI

SIBBI AND THE twins are playing a game of hide-and-seek.

Sibbi hears Finn come down the stairs. He is looking in the girls' bedroom, she thinks. He tiptoes into Dorothy's study, the one room in the house that still makes the children feel like visitors. Like intruders. He doesn't see Sibbi at first. He goes into the room and looks around. He follows the noise. He finds Sibbi behind the curtains.

Sibbi has a permanent marker in her hand. On the wall is a dark, black scribble. Sibbi usually likes to draw girls with eyelashes and love-hearts for mouths, or dogs with fingers and toes, or fat birds sprouting stumpy wings and long stick legs. But this is ugly, babyish drawing.

Sibbi's face is fierce with concentration. The texta in Sibbi's hands is scribbling in smaller and smaller circles.

'Sibbi! What are you doing? It's naughty to draw on the walls!'

Sibbi looks up, her face flushed. She looks at the texta in her hand and drops it on the ground.

'It was an accident,' she says.

She has drawn on herself as well, black lines running up her arms, more black lines straight down, over her eyelids, and down her cheeks.

'You're going to be in big trouble,' Finn says. 'Come on.'

Sibbi lets Finn lead her into the bathroom. She looks at herself in the mirror. 'I know what an endsister is,' she says to Finn. Under the black texta her skin looks yellow. Sickly. *Homesickly*.

'Yeah?' he says, not paying much attention. He begins to scrub at the texta with a wet washer. It doesn't erase.

'It's a kind of a ghost.'

'This isn't coming off. We're going to have to tell Mum.'

Sibbi looks in the mirror. 'I don't look like me.'

'It's just texta. It'll wash off eventually.'

But Sibbi tells him, 'I don't already look like me. That's why I drew on there. Because I didn't look like me anymore. I look like *her*.'

'Like who?'

Sibbi looks at Finn. 'I know,' she says. 'I know what an endsister is.'

ELSE

I CAREFULLY CLOSE the lid of the baby violin. I go to the door of the workshop.

The violin that I held the other day is still sitting there in its case. I remember how it felt to hold it. I remember the electricity of unplayed music fizzing between me and the violin. I close that lid too, like closing the lid of a coffin. It seems wrong to leave it open. I zip up the case.

And then, hardly knowing what I'm doing, I pick up the violin in its case, and strides out the door with it. It is the worst thing I have ever done in my life. But I cannot stop myself from doing it.

Every step is a choice to continue on this path, and yet it's as if I have no choice. I glimpse my reflection in a shop window. I look like a phantom from my own past – Else and the violin – and yet I barely recognise myself at all.

CLANCY

I SPEND ALL day waiting for Pippa to come home from school, but when she does, she has homework. I feel weirdly envious. I sort of miss homework. It's still a few weeks till the summer break, and then holidays. I won't start school till September.

'Remember you and your parents are coming to dinner at our house tonight, though?' she says.

I perk up.

'When's Dad coming home?' I ask Mum. She's staring at her computer screen. She bites her lip. She selects a couple of paragraphs and hits delete. Then she sighs and hits command+Z.

'I wish there was an undo button in real life,' Mum says.

'Mum!'

'What? Sorry. Did you ask me something? I'm working. Oh, your father. Isn't he home? He should be on the next train, I suppose. What time is it?'

'We're having dinner with Pippa and her dad, remember?'

'Yes, yes,' says Mum, but I see alarm in her eyes. She'd obviously forgotten. I wonder if Dad has remembered.

I walk up to the station to meet him coming off the train. I hardly recognise him, blending in with all the other commuters in their business suits and briefcases. He looks like a proper adult. It's hard to imagine him back home building fences, playing dress-ups with Sibbi, chasing birds out of the veggie patch, walking the bounds of Aunty May's land under a big Australian sky.

Home. Strange to think that London was Dad's first home.

'Do you remember living here?' I ask him as we walk down Mortlake Road together.

'Flashes of it,' Dad says. 'I used to play football, soccer of course, not Aussie rules, in the street with other kids.'

'What else?'

'I remember punks in the high street. And Dad – my dad – losing his job at the bank. And then it seemed to me that his job was looking for work, because every day he'd get up early, put on a suit and tie. And then one day I came home from school and all these holiday brochures were on the kitchen table. Uluru (though they called it Ayers Rock back then), the Sydney Opera House, kangaroos hopping along a beach at sunset. And they told me, "Well, Davey. This is Australia, how would you like to live there?" The only thing I knew about Australia was cricket. Greg Chappell, Allan Border, Dennis Lillee, Rod Marsh.'

'And then you moved?'

'Yeah. It was hard on my mum. Not so much on Dad, because he was just happy to be working again. Then Mum got a job as well, in a café, and she was happy too. And I lost my English accent, even my English nickname, Davey. In Australia, I was always Dave.'

Before we go inside Outhwaite House, Dad asks me, 'How's *your* mum today?'

I shrug. 'She never goes anywhere. She just sits at her computer all day.'

'The faster she can finish her PhD, the easier it will be for her to get teaching work over here. She'll be happier when she's working.' But Dad doesn't look that sure about it. 'Maybe we can get her out this weekend. A walk along the river.'

So Dad has noticed that Mum never leaves the house too?

Sibbi is sitting in the middle of the big couch in the lounge room, sinking into the cushions. It looks like it's digesting her. The TV is on and Sibbi is staring at it vacantly.

'Hi, Sibbi,' Dad says.

She blinks up at him. 'Daddy!' she says, but when he leans over to give her a kiss she twists sideways so she can see past him to the screen.

'Shall we turn this off?' he says, picking up the remote.

'No!' Sibbi says. 'I'm watching my shows.'

'Oh, Dave.' Mum comes into the lounge room, towel-drying her hair. She's wearing a dress too. 'Don't turn it off!'

Dad puts the remote down. 'But Sibbi *never* watches TV.'

'What do you expect, Dave? I can't entertain her all the time. There's just not that much for Sibbi to do here when the kids go out and we're both working. Like it or not, television is our new friend.'

I look at Sibbi. Her skin looks pale, doughy, her eyes hollow and dark and her cheeks still streaky with dried-out tears, her body soft and floppy – I find it hard to picture her scrambling up trees, or walking kilometres and kilometres over paddocks and through the bush on the family weekend rambles, or even running down to see Aunty May with a basket of warm rolls fresh from our oven. She has a glazed look on her face, and her fingers are in her mouth, a habit I thought she had given up.

Mum tells me, 'I've asked Else to babysit tonight.'

'Babysit?' says Dad.

'Next door's invited us over for dinner and a drink. You know, Pippa's dad. The architect. Dave, I told you.'

'Pippa?'

'Clancy's friend. The girl next door.'

'Yes. Yes, I remember,' Dad says. 'Clancy has a friend.' He nudges me. 'And she's only got two legs, right? I mean, she's an actual child? Not a dog or a cat or a possum or a fox or a –'

'Bird,' says Sibbi.

'She's a bird?' Dad asks.

Sibbi laughs. 'She's *not* a bird. She's a human people.'

'Why isn't Sibbi coming?'

Mum looks drained. 'We can't take Sibbi. You know how she carries on lately.'

'We always take Sibbi.' Dad looks at me, but I shake my head. Honestly, Sibbi's been such a pain lately, I'd rather not take her either.

'I'll take her to the park tomorrow,' I promise. 'You want to go to the park, right, Sibbi?'

Sibbi shakes her head. 'Nuh-uh.'

'He's a single dad, with an only child. He's not prepared for Sibbi. You know she bit me the other day?'

'And I drawed on the walls,' says Sibbi, brightly. 'And it won't wash out.'

'Oh, Sibbi,' says Dad. 'But you're sorry now, aren't you?'

'Sorry, not sorry. Sorry, not sorry,' says Sibbi.

Dad says, 'I think you are a bit sorry, really.'

'We could just skip it altogether,' says Mum.

'No way!' I say. 'Pippa's dad will have already started cooking. You promised, Mum!'

'Of course we'll come,' says Dad. 'It's a good idea, Olly, hey? Get out and about? Relax, and meet some people? You're right. Else can look after Sibbi.'

Mum doesn't look convinced. 'You two go,' she says. 'I've been thinking I need to rewrite that chapter again. I found a new reference and –'

'Mum, I want you to come,' I say. 'Please.'

'How long has it been since you've spoken to another adult, Olly?' Dad asks.

'What's that supposed to mean?' Mum asks.

'I mean Sibbi's here all day by herself watching television. Who knows what the twins are up to. Else disappears all day. Clancy seems to be spending all his time next door.'

Mum crosses her arms. 'What are you suggesting?'

Dave puts his hands up. 'Look, I'm not trying to pick a fight here. I just think you could do with some company.'

'Look, you were the one who wanted to –'

Sibbi puts her hands over her ears and screams.

'Sibbi!' says Mum. 'Mama and Daddy are trying to have a conversation.'

'I can't hear my show,' says Sibbi.

'Are you two fighting?' Else asks, bored, peering into the lounge room.

'No!' Mum and Dad snap at the same time. Else looks at me and rolls her eyes.

'Whatever.'

'But we are having a *personal* discussion,' Mum says.

'All right, all right, I get the hint. I'll be in my room when you need me. Don't come in without knocking.'

'It's my room too,' Sibbi says.

'Don't remind me.'

I follow Mum and Dad out into the hallway. 'We're still going to Pippa's, aren't we?'

Dad ignores me. He tells Mum, 'My dad grew up here. *His* dad grew up here. Outhwaites have always lived in this house since it was first built.'

Somehow Mum isn't cross anymore. She answers, as if they've been having another conversation all along: 'It's just a house, Dave. At the end of the day, it's just a house.'

'Are we still going to Pippa's?'

'Let me take a shower and get out of this suit,' Dad says. 'Then I'll be ready for dinner next door. I'm looking forward to meeting this real human people friend of yours, Clancy.'

CLANCY

DAD AND JONTY, Pippa's dad, seem to have a fine old time discussing the finer details of inheritance tax, building regulations in London, property law and the value of the Australian dollar against the British pound. Money! Why do grown-ups always want to talk about boring things?

Mum pokes absent-mindedly at her watercress and cheddar tart. She looks tired and a little bored.

'I might just nip in next door and check on Sibbi and Else and the twins,' she says, putting her fork down.

'No!' I say, knowing that if she leaves she'll never come back. 'They're fine.'

Dad sits back in his chair. 'Poor Else can't believe she's moved into this enormous house and she still has to share a bedroom with the baby. Of course, eventually we'll clear out Dorothy's study for Sibbi, but it's a big job.'

Jonty raises an eyebrow. 'Have you thought about going up into the attic?'

'Attic?' asks Dad.

'There is no attic,' Pippa and I say together, quickly.

Jonty raises a finger. 'Ah,' he says. 'Ah, that's what Dorothy used to say. She had an infuriatingly stubborn mental block about it.'

'I wonder why,' says Mum.

'Ghosts, probably,' says Jonty, pouring himself and Dad another glass of wine. Mum covers her glass and shakes her head.

'Ghosts?' says Dad. 'You're not serious!'

'Oh, perfectly serious. Some surveys say as many as three in four Britons believe in ghosts. I come across it all the time in my line of work, renovating historic houses. People are always thinking it's unhappy ghosts that are banging on the pipes, playing haywire with the electrics, thumping on the stairs, pushing things off the shelves. Usually there's a perfectly ordinary explanation, of course, rats or bats or birds, the wind, old warped wood, dodgy wiring, worn-out plumbing.'

'You said *usually*,' I say. '*Usually* there's an ordinary explanation.'

'Well,' says Jonty. 'Sometimes . . .' He takes a sip of wine. 'I mean, I'm not saying I believe in ghosts. But I've certainly seen things I can't explain. I've never been frightened, though, more curious.'

'Was Dorothy frightened?' Dad asks.

Jonty shrugs. 'Just . . . *resistant*. Sort of protective. I'd have taken her for a baked-on history nut, you know, the type that doesn't want anything to change ever, even as the house falls down around them, except I knew her better than that. She had a lively, progressive mind, she loved new ideas, and new things. She just seemed ... disinterested in updating the house, sort of noncommittal, as if was something she might get round to one day.'

'She was busy,' says Pippa. 'That was all.'

Jonty agrees. 'I always had the feeling she'd have liked to move to something smaller and more modern, but she didn't have the heart to give up the family home.'

'I don't like to think of her in that big rattly house all by herself. What a good thing she had you, Pippa,' says Mum. 'You must miss her.'

Pippa smiles gratefully at Mum.

'I don't get it,' says Dad. 'Dorothy lived in that house her whole life. You can't just *un*see a whole attic.'

'Well, there definitely is one. You can see the window from the street if you know what you're looking for. Come upstairs and I'll show you what we've done with ours. The floor plans of this entire row of houses are almost identical.'

When I first heard Jonty worked from home, I thought Pippa meant he sat hunched over a battered laptop at the kitchen table like Mum's always done. But stepping into Jonty's office is like stepping out into an open-plan floor of a city building. All the walls have been removed, so it is one enormous light, lofty space with an open mezzanine floor. Everything is white walls and timber and glass, all of it gleaming. It makes me realise how shabby Outhwaite House is in comparison, like something left over from another century. Which, I suppose, it is.

I walk over to the wall that Pippa's house shares with Outhwaite House's attic and press my ear against it. I don't believe in ghosts. I believe in bats and rats and birds, in creaking branches, and ageing houses. If I can hear anything – a dry rattle, a scraping, scratching sound – well, it must have a perfectly rational explanation.

Dave taps his chin with his finger, thinking. 'That door, on the landing, the one we thought was a locked cupboard. It must lead up to the attic. We could have a look, at least. Maybe Sibbi could move in there. She'd be closer to us. I love the idea of opening it out like this eventually.'

'*More* space?' says Mum, weakly. 'Remember the cottage? Remember how we always said we *preferred* living in small houses, the children all gathered around us?'

'Well, they're growing up,' says Jonty. 'It stands to reason that Else and the boys will need rooms of their own to grow into.'

Pippa rolls her eyes. 'Lots of families in the third world share one room, Daddy.'

Mum frowns. 'I'm just not sure I like the idea of Sibbi alone in an attic. Anyway, it's probably full of boxes and furniture and things. There must be a reason why the door is locked.'

'I can't believe it,' says Jonty. 'I cannot believe you don't want to explore every square inch of that fascinating house.'

'Fascinating,' agrees Mum, wearily. 'But so many *things*. I don't even know where to begin sorting through it. I mean, how do you make meaning of someone's life through their leftover stuff? Everything is important and nothing is.'

'Some of it might be worth quite a bit,' says Jonty. 'It can be hard to tell sometimes which are the more *collectable* pieces.

It would be worth getting an expert in. I can recommend someone. Someone who specialises in deceased estates.'

'What's a deceased estate?' asks Pippa.

'A house where the owner has died,' Dad says.

'It sounds like the house has died,' I say.

'Yes, we ought to do that,' says Mum. 'But no expert can tell me which things Dorothy cared most about, which pen she liked to use, which was her favourite poetry book or cup to drink out of.'

'Yes, I see what you mean,' Jonty says. 'Still, it will all have to be dealt with in due course. Now, there's gooseberry crumble in the oven. Can I tempt you?'

SIBBI

FOR SIBBI, LIVING with the two ghosts, Almost Annie and Hardly Alice, is not that different from living with Else. The ghosts drift silently from room to room, sometimes showing interest in the children, sometimes absorbed in their own thoughts.

Sometimes the ghosts are clear as day to Sibbi; other times they are pale smears against the air. Sibbi has never heard them speak, but she thinks perhaps they speak to each other.

When Sibbi's emotions become too much for her and she gives way to frustration or despair – screaming till she turns red, kicking the walls, drumming her feet on the floor, throwing toys, tearing the sheets from her bed – Hardly Alice hastily retreats, vanishing through walls. Almost Annie, though, will sit nearby and wait Sibbi out, with endless loving patience.

Almost Annie is sitting by Sibbi's bed now, shaking her head, looking worriedly down at Sibbi.

The ghosts do not frighten Sibbi. That would be like being frightened of Else. She is more frightened of the portraits on the walls: stern Victorian ladies and gentlemen frowning down from the walls as if to say *children should be seen and not heard* and *the corn has ears* and *spare the rod, spoil the child.*

Clancy and Pippa came up with a whole list of them as they walked around the portraits: *there's more than one way to skin a cat, you can't get blood out of a stone, don't get your knickers in a knot* and Mama taught Pippa: *I hope your chickens turn into emus and kick your dunny down.*

Worst of all of them, as far as Sibbi is concerned, is *don't throw the baby out with the bathwater.* Oh, that poor, wet baby, tumbling out into the bin. She can't bear it.

Sibbi screams again and pummels her feet on the wall. She can't even remember why she is angry, but the anger comes and comes in waves, building and building and never going away, like bees have built a nest in her chest and are buzzing angrily so she can't hear or see her thoughts anymore, only bees, a black whirling rage of bees.

Else bangs on the door. 'Let me in or I'm going next door to get Mum and she'll be furious.'

'Sorry not sorry,' Sibbi howls. 'Sorry not sorry.'

And she listens to the sound of Else's footsteps, stomping down the stairs. She hears the front door open and slam shut. And she buries her face in her pillow and screams and screams and screams.

CLANCY

PIPPA HAS A huge map of the world hanging on the wall in her room. It is still strange to visualise myself in the top left corner, that where I stand is within that unfamiliar shape high up on the top of the world. The shape of Australia is so familiar to me, I could draw it freehand with my eyes closed.

I look at England. France is so close you can go to Paris for the day in the fast train; Pippa told me that if you leave at breakfast you can be home for supper. Belgium, the Netherlands, Denmark, Germany – they all look intimately close. Pippa goes abroad every summer with one of her parents. This year she's going to Spain with her mum and stepfather. Dad says it's cheaper to go to Europe from England than for Victorians to go on a Queensland holiday in Australia, but I suppose everything is expensive when you're a family of seven.

Pippa stands on her bed to reach England, and traces her finger all the way down to Australia.

'I'd love to go to Australia,' she says. 'I want to see all the animals you told me about. The swamp wallabies, the sugar gliders . . . pobblebonks.' I've told her all about the animals from home. 'Do you miss it?'

'Not always. It comes and goes in flashes, but most of the time, I'm just . . . *here* and *now*. Living in the moment.'

'I would miss it. I *do* miss it, even though I've never been there.'

'Do you miss living with your mum?'

'*No.* I mean, I love Mummy. I wish I could see her every day, and not just on Skype. But the school I went to when I lived at her house during the week was awful. Everybody was bullying everybody. Kids bullying kids. Teachers bullying kids. Teachers bullying teachers. Kids bullying teachers. It was a nightmare. With Daddy everything is calm. And Kingsley is too. There are lots of kids like me, kids who don't fit in boxes.'

Just then there was a bang at the door and voices downstairs.

'Sorry,' I say. 'My family is not calm.'

'Wait here,' Pippa says. 'I'll snitch us some crumble and find out what's going on.'

She comes back without crumble and reports anxiously, 'Else is here because Sibbi is throwing a massive tantrum in her room. Your mum is cross with Else for leaving Sibbi and the twins at home alone. And Dave and Daddy have drunk all the wine and they're going over to Outhwaite House to open up the attic!'

'What?'

'Do you think we should go over there? They might hurt themselves. Daddy can be a bit silly when he's been drinking.'

'Do you believe in ghosts?' I ask Pippa.

Pippa thought. 'Both my dad and my mum do, in different ways. But I'm a scientist. I need evidence. There's a lot more dead people than alive ones – surely if ghosts existed we'd see them all the time. What about you? Do you believe in them?'

'I believe in the creeps. There's a sound evolutionary basis for the creeps. An instinct for danger. An internal early warning system. That door definitely gives me the creeps.'

'Me too,' Pippa admits.

'Come on. I suppose in the interests of science we should be there when the door opens.'

CLANCY

PIPPA AND I CAN hear Sibbi howling in the bedroom. 'Are you sure it's okay for me to be here?' Pippa whispers.

'Oh, this is normal,' I say. 'Pretty normal anyway.'

Mum taps on the door. 'Sibbi? Sibbi, love. Let Mama in.'

'I know what an endsister is,' Sibbi howls.

'What *is* an endsister?' Pippa whispers.

'According to Sibbi, it's a kind of ghost.'

'Interesting,' says Pippa.

In contrast with Sibbi, the dads are in a *very* silly mood. Dad tries every key in the lock.

'Let me try,' Jonty says. 'I'm a professional.'

He jiggles the keys in the locks too, but none of them work.

The twins look on, Oscar with excitement, Finn with trepidation.

'Kick the door down, Dad!' Oscar says.

Sibbi's wails get louder.

'What's she saying?' Jonty asks us. '*Endsister*?'

'It's a kind of a ghost,' Pippa tells him.

'I know! I *know*!' Sibbi howls. 'I know what an endsister is.'

'There are no ghosts in this house,' says Dad. 'It's like a rule.' And he and Jonty giggle.

'Have you got a screwdriver?' Jonty asks.

Dad tells Oscar to get out. 'There'll be one in the toolshed.'

'It's dark out there!' Finn says.

'So?' says Oscar. He scampers down the stairs, relishing the task of a good dig around the toolshed in the dark.

'Are you really going to shut Sibbi in there?' Finn asks.

'It's not a punishment,' Dad says, while Jonty wiggles another key, pressing his ear against the door and listening. 'This way, she'll be closer to me and Mum. It's time Else had a room of her own.'

Oscar comes back with the screwdriver, Mum following him.

'What are you going to do?' Mum asks Dad.

'Oh, don't ruin it, Mum,' Oscar says. 'This is brilliant.'

'I'll be gentle,' promises Dad. 'I'll just try . . .' He wiggles the screwdriver into the lock.

And the lock clicks.

ALMOST ANNIE
AND HARDLY ALICE

'WHAT IS IT?' Almost Annie asks Hardly Alice. 'What are we so afraid of? You've been here longer than me. Do you *know* what's behind that door?'

'It wants –' Alice moans.

'What does it want?' Almost Annie begs.

Alice steps towards the door and Almost Annie steps away. 'I must check on the child,' Annie quails, and she turns and flees down the stairs. But Alice can't bear to look away.

The door rattles. *Rage. Disappointment. Despair. Sorrow. Sorrow. Dust. Dust. Dust.*

CLANCY

Downstairs Sibbi's crying has quietened. Else has stopped banging on the nursery door. Sibbi must have finally unlocked it.

The house is silent. Pippa steps closer to me. It feels like the whole house has stopped to take a breath, like someone gasping good sweet fresh air the moment before they the sink beneath the surface of a weedy, murky pond.

'There,' says Dad. 'I've done it. I'm not quite sure *how* – it's almost like it wasn't locked after all. But we're in.'

The attic door swings open, revealing a narrow wooden staircase. All we can see at the top is deep, textured darkness. It seems, at first, to be moving. A swirling, breathing, living sort of dark, with intentions of its own.

A trick of the light, I think. *A trick of the dark.*

Jonty, Dad and Oscar peer up the stairs.

I glance over at Pippa, whose eyes are wide with alarm. And to her left for a moment I see Else out of the corner of my eye. At least, I think it's Else and that Else is frightened, but when I blink, it's not Else but some old-fashioned girl with a narrow face, the same sort of sad-angry face as Else's. But then I look a third time and there's no one there at all.

Dad says, uncertainly, 'See? Nothing to worry about.'

One of Sibbi's ghosts, I think. And then I feel silly.

'Dad's right,' I say to Pippa. 'There's no such thing as ghosts.'

'Did I say that?' Dad says. 'No such thing as ghosts?'

'It's okay, Pippa,' Jonty says. 'Nothing to be scared of here. See?'

From downstairs Else screams, a head-splitting, ear-shattering, skull-cracking scream.

ELSE

'LOOK WHAT SHE'S done!' I shriek, as Olly and Dave rush into the nursery. 'Look what that monster has done!'

A man I don't know – Pippa's dad, I suppose, since Pippa stands unhappily behind him – pops his head into the room and sees me, Sibbi in Dave's arms, the good scissors, and the violin on the floor with every string cut, and says, with typical English unflappability, 'We'll be off then. Do pop round any time.'

Toodle-pip, old chum.

I try to kill him with a death stare, but he toodle-pips with no discernible harm, though Pippa appears to be suffering.

Sibbi writhes and flails in Dave's arms. She tries to hit his face. He holds down her hands and looks at Olly in shock. Sibbi squirms, screaming, 'I *hate* her! I hate having a sister. I never asked to have a sister.'

'I never asked for *you* to be born,' I hurl back at Sibbi as Dave pulls her from the room. '*I* was here *first*.'

'Else, stop shouting at Sibbi and look at me,' Olly says, with irritating calm. 'Whose violin is this? Where did it come from?'

'It's mine. It's not mine. I . . . I borrowed it.'

'From who?'

'Lev Starman.'

Olly blinks. 'What's a Star Man?'

'You wouldn't understand! She's wrecked it and I'm the one who'll get into trouble. She gets away with everything. She's such a spoiled little brat.'

'I'm trying to understand what you're telling me.'

'He's a violin-maker. Oh, it's too hard to explain. Mum, you have to take it back to him for me. I'll . . . I'll pay for any damage. But I can't go back there.'

Olly sits down on Sibbi's bed. 'When you say you borrowed it . . . Else, tell me the truth. Did you steal this violin?'

'No!' I say and I sort of believe myself. 'Of course I didn't. I'm not a thief. I'm not.'

'So this Star Man, he knows you have his violin?'

I press my hands against my eyes, unable to look at Olly. 'Not exactly. But he did say no one would notice a violin missing from his workshop. And then he showed me this particular violin. Maybe he wanted . . . I mean, he could have been saying . . . He did say I could play one.'

'Else,' Olly says gently. 'I'm going to ask you again. Did you steal this violin?'

I nod, releasing a long, shuddering sob. 'I never even got the chance to play it.'

Olly puts her arms around me while I weep.

'Why?' Olly asks. 'Why are you so unhappy? Do you really hate it here that much?'

But I can't blame London. I was unhappy in Hong Kong, and in Melbourne. I was unhappy before Aunty May got sick, before Dorothy Outhwaite died. It was the Mozart. Was it the just the Mozart?

'What if –?' My voice falters. I can't say it. *What if I'm not good enough to play professionally? What if I'm ordinary?* I look at the broken violin and at the good scissors. What if the *music* inside me is broken like the violin and nothing will ever fix it?

'Why did you leave your violin behind in Australia, Else?'

'I – I wanted to know who I am without it.'

'And who are you?'

I say nothing, but I've known the whole time, ever since Hong Kong anyway. I recognised myself at the bird market, looking at that bird in the cage. I'm a song trapped in a chest in a cage in a city. That's who I am without my violin.

SIBBI

Daddy sits halfway up the stairs, holding Sibbi in his arms until she sobs herself out. She looks up at Daddy as if she has just remembered him.

'You open the door?'

'Yes,' Daddy says. 'I opened the door.'

'Nothing to be scared of?' Sibbi asks.

'You don't have to go up there,' Finn says, peering down. 'You can sleep in our room.'

Oscar appears beside him at the top of the stairs. 'She can*not*!'

'Up we go,' says Daddy, standing with Sibbi still in his arms. 'Up we go and look. Nothing to be scared of, I promise.'

Daddy carries Sibbi up to the attic. Oscar scurries ahead, clambering up the steep staircase on all fours.

'You'll need to climb up yourself, Sibbi,' says Daddy. 'I can't carry you up those stairs. You go first and I'll come up behind.'

The pitched roof in the middle of the attic is high enough for Daddy to stand up, but low at the east and west walls.

Still, it's high enough for Sibbi to stand up in any spot in the room. Surprisingly, there is very little up here, a few paintings stacked against the wall, some furniture draped in sheets. It's very dark, only lit by the light coming up from the landing and some borrowed light from the street lamps outside (the city never gets dark). There are windows to the north and south, Daddy points out, so the room would be bright in the daytime, and an electrician could easily run wires up here, it wouldn't be a big job. In fact, with a lick of paint and the right furniture, it would be a perfect child's bedroom, lofty and spacious, yet cosy and playful.

'If Sibbi doesn't want this room, can I have it?' Oscar says.

'It's Sibbi's room,' Daddy says. 'This room will be for Sibbi.'

'Sibbi's room,' says Sibbi.

Finn stands on the stairs, sticking his head up into the attic to look around. 'Why is the furniture wearing sheets?'

'To catch the dust,' says Daddy.

'Then why are they so clean?' asks Finn.

'Huh,' says Daddy. The sheets are bright and luminous, catching the light.

'It's not fair,' says Oscar. 'Why does Sibbi get a room of her own? Why do Finn and I have to share? Just because we're twins.'

'I like sharing,' says Finn.

'I don't,' says Oscar. 'I hate it.'

'This room,' says Sibbi, 'is for Sibbi.' She is pale in the attic, and very, very small.

ELSE

'I can't take the violin back for you,' Olly says. 'You have to do it yourself.'

'What? Why? That's not fair!'

'But you see, it *is* fair, Else. Fair is exactly what it is,' Olly insists. 'I can come with you, if you want. But I won't be doing you any favours if I step in for you.'

'What about Sibbi? Are you going to punish *her*?' A darkness passes through the room and enters my heart. The darkness is invisible, but it's real, as cold as the blades of the good scissors. It hurts my chest. Olly puts her hand on my arm, but I stiffen at her touch.

'I'm tired now,' I say, coldly, turning away from her.

'We can take the violin back tomorrow. You and me *and* Sibbi. And Sibbi can apologise for what she's done. After we go to Harrods for the uniforms. Sweetheart, it won't be so bad. Better to face it head on.'

I close my eyes. I don't want to face it.

'Else,' says Olly. 'Are you sure you want to go to this

school? Lady Emily Hartington? Is that part of what's making you miserable? It's not too late to change your mind.'

It hurts, this tight gasping pain in my chest. Everything hurts. This is my punishment, but is anyone going to punish Sibbi?

'Can you get out of my room now?'

Downstairs there's an enormous crash. 'What now?' sighs Olly.

But I don't care. It's nothing to do with me.

CLANCY

I MEET DAD, Mum and the twins downstairs in the kitchen. A shelf has come loose from the wall and slid downwards, and all the contents have fallen to the floor.

'This night is turning out awesome,' Oscar yelps.

'The Royal Doulton serving plate!' gasps Mum. 'And the Wedgewood coffee service.' Her eyes fill with tears.

'What happened?' Dad asks.

'I don't know. It just fell.'

'At least none of the kids were in here.'

'Oh, Dave. All these beautiful things.'

'What a mess.'

'Oh, poor Dorothy. Poor, poor Dorothy. How long have those things been there, safe in her keeping? And now they're gone. Just like that.'

'It's not our fault,' Oscar says. 'We didn't do it.'

'I suppose not,' says Mum.

'Come on kids, it's time for bed,' Dad says. 'Where's Sibbi? It's getting late. It's time for bed.'

'I don't think we can put Sibbi in with Else tonight,' Mum says, 'She's still so angry.'

'Sibbi's going to sleep in the attic,' says Oscar. 'It's totally spooky up there!'

'Oh, Dave. No.'

'Well, not tonight, obviously,' Dad says, shooting Oscar a look. 'Sib can sleep in our room tonight. Come on, I think we could all use some sleep. We'll sort out this mess in the morning.'

'You go ahead,' Mum says. 'I won't sleep until I've cleaned this up.'

THE ATTIC DOOR, having finally opened, will not properly close, so it swings slightly ajar.

Carried by a bitter wind straight out of the attic, bad dreams float through Outhwaite House like black balloons.

Sibbi is in the kitchen of the little house on the hill back home in Australia. There's a shadow hanging over the valley. There's a new baby crying, and everyone is rushing around, grabbing things for the baby. Hardly Alice and Almost Annie are in the dream too. Hardly Alice says to Sibbi, 'See, I told you it would be like this.' Almost Annie shakes her head. 'It's all your fault, Sibbi. You were so naughty they had to have another baby.' Sibbi looks down to Aunty May's house. Aunty May stands at the road, waving at cars driving past with both arms. She has several suitcases all around her, like she is going on a long journey.

It is the first day at Clancy's new school, which looks half like his old school and half like the Natural History Museum. Clancy sees Pippa in a crowd and calls out, but Pippa merely glances back over her shoulder and keeps moving away from him. The other children throng between them, with blank, unsmiling faces and he pushes through, desperate to get to Pippa. When he does finally catch up to her, it's in a large classroom, but there are no desks or chairs. He taps her on the shoulder and she turns around. 'Love,' she says, and starts swaying her hips from side to side, like she's dancing. Clancy sees that all the other children in the classroom are also girls and they all start swinging their hips, with their strange, serious faces. 'Love,' they drone, swaying three times. 'Love,' they say again. Over and over, saying 'love' and swaying their hips, swinging their long ponytails, never smiling.

Finn has found the box of family photographs. He's rummaging around inside, looking for pictures of himself, but all he finds are photographs of Oscar. Oscar swimming, Oscar running, Oscar playing cricket and football. Oscar smiling straight into the camera. 'What's the difference?' Else asks. 'It's the same thing, isn't it?'

Oscar is playing sport but there's no ball and he's not sure of the rules. Everyone's running around on the field, and he runs with them. All the boys shoulder each other out of the way, jostling each other. Unprepared for a flying tackle, Oscar gets knocked off his feet. 'You lose,' the tackling boy tells Oscar. 'You have to get off the field now.' Oscar goes to the sidelines and the coach tells him that he can't play without his twin, but when he looks around, it's not Finn running out on the field, it's Sibbi.

Olly is standing in the lounge room of Outhwaite House, which is very formally furnished. There is a fire in the fireplace. She is seventeen years old, and wearing a straight, sensible grey skirt and a cream-coloured silk blouse. Her father is standing by the piano. He says, 'Don't be foolish, Dorothy. That is the last I will hear of it.' And Olly says, 'But I've almost finished my doctoral thesis, Papa.' Her father says, 'I find that very hard to believe, young lady, you've hardly written a word.' He hands her an envelope. She opens it up and inside is her PhD thesis, handwritten on thin sheets of paper. She can see that it's not enough, but she looks at her father and says, 'You stupid man, can't you see I've written on both sides of the pages?' He roars, furious, and sends her out. In the hallway she leans against the wall, and tears her thesis into little pieces. Instantly she regrets it. She's on hands and knees, sweeping the pieces of paper towards her, but it's too late, the damage is done. Only it's not a thesis. It's a love letter and a goodbye.

Dave is in the front room of Outhwaite House, with the curtains drawn. There are two coffins, a long one and a short one. 'Well, it was a cruel time,' Olly says, slipping her arm into Dave's. 'No antibiotics. No immunisations. Filthy streets and hospitals. Children died all the time. I'm thinking about writing a book about it. It's terribly interesting.'

'But who's in the coffins?' Dave asks.

'Oh, David,' says Olly. 'Honestly. Who do you think?' She turns to him, smiling. 'We're so lucky,' says Olly. 'We're so frightfully, frightfully *lucky*.'

Else is standing in the road. It is Mortlake Road, but not how it is now; it's how it must have been more than a hundred years ago, before cars and electric lights. She's wearing all black, Victorian mourning clothes; she's buttoned, sheathed, laced and bound, layers upon layers of restrictive garments, from neck to knee and she can hardly breathe, but that might be because she is weeping. There's a funeral procession – a tiny child-sized coffin being carried down the street. The girl standing next to Else digs her nails into her arm. Else recognises her as one of Sibbi's ghosts. She says to Else, 'You never wanted a sister. Now look what you've done.'

'It wasn't me,' Else protests. She looks down at her hands and finds she is holding Prince George's tiny violin.

'Every wrong note was hurting her,' says Almost Annie, sorrowfully. 'It's all your fault.'

ELSE

I WAKE SUDDENLY to the sound of a horn blaring.

I'm standing in the middle of Mortlake Road. I'm wearing the clothes I went to bed in: T-shirt, loose gym shorts. The night air is cold on my skin. A horn blares again. I leap out of the way of a black cab coming towards me, with no intention, apparently, of actually slowing down.

'You all right?' There are two guys walking up the street, both wearing tight tops, tight pants, like they've been out dancing.

'I'm fine,' I tell them.

For a moment the dream takes over again and the street flickers back to Old Mortlake Road. I remember the coffin and shiver.

'You lost?' they ask me.

'I must have been sleepwalking,' I say.

'Hey, that's okay,' one of them says. 'Sleepwalking's *cool*. Only the best people continue their adventures in their sleep.'

His partner frowns, concerned. 'You sure you're okay?'

I nod. I've reoriented myself, Outhwaite House is behind me and the front door is open. The two guys walk up the street holding hands. As one leans his head on the other's shoulder, I've never felt more alone.

ELSE

AT BREAKFAST I can barely stand to be in the same room as any of my family. I eat two bites of my Weetabix, Sibbi eats half a bite of hers and starts whimpering, and Olly joylessly works her way through a bowl of rolled oats and yoghurt.

We step out into the street. Olly flinches when the door to Outhwaite House slams behind her.

'Come on. Keep up.' I stride down the street ahead of them.

'What's that smell?' asks Olly.

'I don't smell anything,' I snap back over my shoulder. But it's probably the plastic bags full of rubbish on the streets, because they don't seem to have a proper bin collection here. Though it's drizzling, the air is oddly warm and the rain feels slightly greasy. Olly and Sibbi look pale and shaky, as though the colour of home is slowly seeping out of them. Instead of that arousing my sympathies, it makes me feel even crosser, especially with Olly. The rest of us have adjusted. Why can't she?

Olly keeps tight hold of Sibbi's hand, though Sibbi squirms and tries to pull away. Olly fumbles with the credit card, trying to buy a ticket. It's me who has to explain how it's done. Olly sits back passively, clutching Sibbi as I watch the names of stations slide past us.

At Hammersmith I stand up. 'We change here for the Piccadilly line,' I tell Olly, and she leaps up in a panic even though the train hasn't so much as opened its doors yet.

'Let's stay together,' Olly keeps gasping as we walk to the other platform. She tries to take hold of my arm but I pull away. We board safely. I sit away from Olly and Sibbi, holding the violin case on my lap. I watch my reflection in the opposite window, pretending I don't belong with Olly and Sibbi. I catch sight of Olly's reflection as she reaches up to push her hair out of her face. Olly has always looked young for her age, but now her face looks pinched and pale and unhappy. Middle-aged. My mother looks middle-aged. I feel no pity. Only rage.

I look strange too. I am a stranger to myself. My outside doesn't match up with my insides. My face appears calm and still, but inside I am churning with anger.

'Get off here,' I bark, as the train pulls into Knightsbridge.

Mortifyingly Olly stops to ask someone for directions, but I tug her away.

'We don't need directions. We follow the signs.' I point to one that says *Harrods*. I wave my Oyster card, still in my wallet, at the gate and it opens. Olly fumbles to get out her own card, and then pulls Sibbi hurriedly through the gate with her, again as if they might get separated. Sibbi cries out,

'You're hurting me.' People turn around to glare at Olly and I try to disappear.

'Sorry, sweetie.' Olly loosens her grip, but she doesn't let go. Olly is supposed to be the grown-up, the one in charge, but she seems entirely diminished by London, and even more so by the opulence of Harrods.

'For heaven's sake,' I say. 'It's only a department store.'

I march up to someone serving behind a counter and ask for directions to school uniforms. We take the escalators up to the fourth floor. Olly gazes around like a tourist, but she seems to take no pleasure in the architecture, or the golden Egyptian statue, or the gleaming floors of designer goods, toys, manchester. Champagne flutes for ten thousand pounds apiece. I know what Olly will be thinking. She hates luxury.

'*Don't. Touch. Anything,*' Olly hisses to Sibbi, who looks pale and small.

Meanwhile I am fascinated by the song of the expensive things, the high-pitched humming of diamond-studded goblets, of little cakes decorated with real gold leaf, of a richness of objects beyond my imagination. I want to touch *everything*, try on the hats, drape scarves and necklaces around myself, cloud myself in perfume, slip between the sheets of beds on display. I want to wear Harrods like a costume, and become someone else entirely.

Sibbi pulls at Olly's hand as we sail up past the toy department. 'Look at the castle. Look at the teddy! I want to see the big teddy.' Sibbi tugs, but Olly holds on tight and says, 'Shush, Sibbi. Later.'

In the school uniform department, it is not simply a matter of trying on clothes. First I must be measured.

I stand stiff and embarrassed while the woman pulls the tape measure around my bust.

'You can put your violin here if you like.'

I hadn't realised I was still holding it.

'Do you play?' the saleswoman asks, wrapping the tape measure around my waist. 'Are you any good?'

'It's not mine,' I answer shortly. 'I'm returning it today.'

The woman sticks her head out of the curtain. 'Will she require the orchestra uniform?' she asks Olly.

'Orchestra uniform?' Olly sounds vaguely panicky, like the woman is speaking a language Olly doesn't understand.

'She'll need the summer skirt, two shirts at least, a blazer, a V-neck jumper and a boater. Lacrosse uniform?'

'I . . . I don't know.'

'And do you want her fitted for a winter uniform now too?'

'How much is all this going to cost?' Olly asks.

'Shall we begin with the summer uniform?' the woman says, kindly and without judgement. 'And you can wait and see about the rest.'

'Why are we still so poor?' I demand loudly. 'We've inherited this big house and all that stuff, I don't get it.'

'We'll talk about it later,' Olly says through the curtain. 'We're not poor,' she reassures the saleswoman with the tape measure. 'We were *never* poor,' she tells me. 'You don't know what it even means to be poor. We've always had food to eat and somewhere to sleep. We've always been safe and warm.'

'Quite right, dear,' says the saleswoman, who is at least twenty years older than Olly. 'Young 'uns today don't know what it is to go without, do they?'

I seal my mouth shut, quietly fuming.

For a moment I think the saleswoman is going to stay with me and watch me try the things on, but she finally leaves me alone with the various garments. I step into the knee-length skirt, and button up the modest lavender shirt. With black tights and school shoes, I'll look more like I'm dressed for a boring office job than school. The skirt is loose enough that it doesn't show any curves but tight enough that I won't be able to stride comfortably in it – the sort of girly attire I've avoided most of my life. Even in orchestra I was allowed to wear pants.

The girl in the mirror is, and is not quite, me. She is an approximation. She is Harrods. She is Lady Jane Whatsit. She is Someone Else.

I come out of the change room to show Olly. Olly shrugs. 'You're the one who has to wear it. What do *you* think?'

'It's a uniform,' I say. 'I'm not supposed to like it.'

The woman with the tape measure brings Sibbi out of the change room. 'What do you think, Mother?' says the woman, seeming misty-eyed herself. 'I do like to see a little girl in a proper school uniform.'

Sibbi wears a pleated skirt, a shirt with a collar, a tartan tie and a buttoned-up cardigan.

What's happened to Sibbi? It's not just the uniform. Sibbi's whole self is changed. Paler and weaker. This little English child, scrawny and pasty, could never climb a tree or spin around and around under an expansive Australian sky. Some quality of Sibbi – her very Sibbiness – has been turned down, like turning down the volume of a television. There is something curiously flat about her face, like she is not quite a girl but a very good likeness of a girl.

London is pulling all of us apart in all directions, but I suddenly realise it is physically *hurting* Sibbi to be here.

'They grow up so fast,' the woman with the tape measure says.

'Do they?' says Olly. 'Yes, I suppose they do.'

Olly! So vague, so insular and withdrawn, as if everything that happens to her happens deep within, somewhere we children can't see.

In the change room, I strip off the uniform and pull my own street clothes back on. Suddenly I want to be out of Harrods. I've tried it on, and now I just want to get away as fast as I can. I want to get Sibbi away too. I want to take Sibbi to a park, to a big expanse of green and run with her and shout and climb. I want to see Sibbi *play*.

But then I remember the violin. I pick it up. I have to return it. I have to return the violin, and buy the uniform and go to the Lady Emily Hartington School for Girls. This is the tight little life I have made for myself, the life I have bound and laced myself into, and there's no way back, no seam to unpick without everything unravelling around me.

SIBBI

KNOCK KNOCK. WHO'S there? Mirror. Mirror who?

The schoolgirl looks at Sibbi. She is Sibbi and she is not Sibbi and Sibbi does not have the black forever texta to scribble her out. If she had the sharp scissors she would cut cut cut. Cut Sibbi's hair. Cut cut cut. Cut Sibbi's school uniform. Cut cut cut. Cut the measuring tape of the helper lady. But Mama took the sharp scissors and carried them away.

Sibbi takes off the schoolgirl clothes and lays them on the floor in the shape of a girl. Sibbi thinks it is a good girl. Sibbi thinks it is a naughty girl in the shape of a good girl.

Sibbi puts on her blue shorts and red T-shirt and brown sandals and looks in the mirror again.

Knock knock. Who's there? Nobody. Nobody who? Nobody nobody.

She walks out of the change rooms. Mama is just over there and the helper lady with the tape measure is plussing all the numbers of the things they have to buy. Olly will be ages because grown-ups always talk and Sibbi is ready *now*, ready to see the toys.

ELSE

OLLY IS AT the counter, her face tense as the woman adds up the purchases. She glances up at me.

'Where's Sibbi?' she asks.

'Isn't she with you?'

'She must still be getting her shoes on, can you hurry her along?'

'Why do *I* have to?'

I go back to the change room.

'Sibbi?' I call out. I tweak open the curtain. 'Come on, time to go.' But Sibbi isn't there. The uniform is laid out on the floor, empty.

I feel a tight, sick squeeze. It's not like Sibbi's never wandered off before, but this is Harrods, a huge department store with floors and floors. This is *London*, a sprawling city, a foreign land, far from the Australian hills Sibbi has been roaming since she learned to walk. There's no kind Aunty May keeping an eye on her as she trots up and down the kangaroo tracks.

'Mum!' I call out. 'She's not here.'

Olly and the saleswoman look at each other in shock.

'Sibbi!' Olly calls. She and I call for Sibbi, looking around the clothing stands and displays. 'Sibbi! Sibbi!' Other shoppers look up, annoyed or curious, but none offer to help.

'Excuse me,' says Olly, tapping the arm of a passing woman. 'Have you seen a little girl? Four years old and ...' The elderly shoppers shake their heads and move away, the woman rubbing her arm where Olly made contact.

I try with someone else. 'Excuse me, have you seen my sister? She's this high, wearing, um ...' I can't remember what Sibbi was wearing. All I can see is Sibbi in her school uniform, little sickly Sibbi.

'She'll turn up, love,' the lady says. 'She'll be in among the toys, no doubt.'

But the more I look, the more Sibbi is not anywhere.

The saleswoman picks up the phone and speaks quickly and sharply into it. An announcement comes over the loudspeaker.

'Good morning, ladies and gentlemen, and welcome to Harrods. We have a missing girl in the store, four years old, wearing a red T-shirt, blue shorts and brown sandals. If you see her please contact a member of staff. Thank you.'

Olly says, 'You go up, I'll go down.'

'What if we can't find her?' I say. 'What if –?'

'Stop,' Olly snaps. She closes her eyes, takes a breath, then says, 'Let's just look, okay? We need to keep our cool. We'll see more if we're calm. Breathe.'

This was so Olly. If I lose a library book or Dave can't find the car keys, she will say, 'Stress narrows your focus. Breathe and be calm. Stay open to all possibilities. The lost thing will reappear.'

I go up the escalator. My knees tremble as I climb to get up faster, nudging past other shoppers. I look around the crowded floor, full of shoppers and shoes on display and, well, *things*. So many useless things. I can't imagine wanting any of it now.

I ask people if they've seen Sibbi. One rather crotchety old man says, 'You should call the police. Leave it to the authorities. Don't want to delay with a case like this.'

His wife tugs at him. 'Come away, Frank. You're frightening the girl.'

I am looking but I cannot see. Every minute that Sibbi is missing is another minute that Sibbi could be further away. All the awful possibilities crowd into my mind – Sibbi snatched by a stranger, run over by a car, wandering and wandering, more lost and frightened by the minute. The Sibbi in the school uniform – pale, diminished – haunts me.

I am supposed to be angry with Sibbi, but the fury is gone now. Did Sibbi run away because of me and the violin? Have I driven Sibbi away? When was the last time I took Sibbi anywhere, or played with her, or smiled, or said even one kind word? Could this be all my fault?

Stress narrows your focus. Breathe and be calm.

Breathe and be calm.

I stop in my tracks. I close my eyes and take a deep breath. And when I open them, it's to see a girl in a Harrods uniform, not much older than me, rushing towards me.

SIBBI

THE ESCALATOR GLIDES Sibbi's body down down down and Sibbi lives inside her body. Sibbi watches her feet, and when it gets to the end, she doesn't step off, she lets the movement of the escalator slowly push her off and then a man behind bumps, and a woman bumps *him* and they are all cross with Sibbi.

Everybody has a body. Nobody doesn't have a body.

Sorry not sorry. Sorry not sorry, her little stepping sandals say on the polished floors.

At first Sibbi is excited to see boxes and boxes of the toys she loves from her TV shows at home. But she doesn't like the faces. They have bodies, but there is no one inside their bodies to think their thoughts.

'Excuse me,' she tries to say to a lady passing by, but the lady doesn't hear her. She wants someone to lift the giant teddy down so she can give it a hug.

'Excuse me.'

'Where's your mother, little girl?' booms a big voice, but the man doesn't stop to hear her answer.

It's no use trying to talk to grown-ups. She sits down and waits for Mama to find out where she is.

ELSE

'Are you Else?' the shop assistant says. 'Your sister's found. Your mum's with her in the toy section, I'll take you there if you like.'

I literally feel my knees buckle under me. All the air goes out of me. I actually start to cry, in front of this strange girl. After weeks – months – of holding it in, now the tears leak out.

'Ah, go on then,' the Harrods girl says. 'Happy tears never hurt anyone.'

I'm scared now I've started I won't be able to stop, but the tears dry up quite quickly. A flash flood.

Downstairs, Olly is holding Sibbi's hand tightly.

'Let's go and get something to eat,' says Olly.

We go to the tearoom on the second floor. Olly clutches Sibbi's hand tightly. I wish for a fleeting moment that Olly would hold my hand too. I still have a case of the serious *what ifs*, my brain still playing out various scenarios.

We order the British afternoon tea special: Earl Grey and

crumpets and lemonade for Sibbi. She rests her head on her arms, watching the bubbles rise to the surface.

'When we inherited the house,' I say, 'I thought it was like winning the lottery.'

Olly shrugs. 'Winning the lottery is probably not always everything you think it's going to be either.'

'Everything's so different here.'

'Different better or different worse?' Olly asks.

'What do you think?'

Olly makes a face.

'You're obviously not happy,' I say.

'I've hardly given it a good go, though, have I, Else?'

'You didn't want to come!'

'I'm just homesick. I mean, it's not fatal. It will pass.' Olly tries to look convincing, and fails. She finishes her tea. 'I can't face going back upstairs to pay for the uniforms. Would you mind if we came back another day?'

'Sure,' I say, hugely relieved that we haven't bought the uniform. 'Let's do that. But I'm not coming home with you now. I have to go and return this violin. Will you be able to get home okay?'

'I can manage,' Olly says, though she looks nervous. 'You don't want me to come with you? Help explain?'

'No. It's something I need to do on my own.'

ELSE

LEV STARMAN OPENS the door. He does not seem surprised to see me.

I hold out the instrument. 'I took it. And I'm so sorry. I wasn't going to keep it, I just wanted to play it. And then my sister cut the strings. She cut them with the good scissors. All the strings.'

'Come in, but wait. I am seeing somebody. Ms Joanna Black.'

Lev Starman returns to his customer and the violin that sits on the table in front of him. Else can see that it has a long crack right down the front.

'I will have to disassemble the instrument,' Starman tells the woman.

'No!'

'It is what must happen in a case like this. You have to repair it from the inside, it cannot be repaired from the outside.' Lev Starman looks at me. 'You can restring a violin?' he asks, abruptly.

I nod.

'There are strings in the box there.'

I rummage in the box and finds the four strings I need, coiled in their paper packages. I thread the first string into the peg and begin winding.

'Will it sound the same?' Ms Black asks.

'Never.'

'Oh,' Ms Black hides her face.

'It will not sound like it did when it was new,' says Starman. 'It will retain its memory of you, but this fall is part of its history now. Maybe it retains the memory of this fall too.'

Ms Black continues to look worried.

'All will be well,' Starman assures her. 'I'll get the paperwork.'

I thread and wind the next string. Joanna Black looks up and smiles. 'Did you play it?'

'Sorry?'

'What's your name?'

'Else.'

'Did you play the violin before your sister cut the strings, Else?'

'Oh. No. No, I didn't.'

'Hm,' says Ms Black. 'That's a shame. I have a tuner in my handbag if you want to tune the strings.'

'Thanks,' I say. I use the tuner to find A, then, by habit, I tune the rest of the violin by ear.

'Play something now,' invites Ms Black. 'Anything you like.'

I freeze. All I can think of, all I can see swimming in front of my eyes like fish, are the notes for the Mozart piece, the piece I could never get right.

'It's been a while,' I tell Ms Black.

Ms Black shrugs. 'Did Mr Starman ever tell you that the world is not waiting for you to play the violin?'

'Yeah!' I say. 'Actually, he did.'

'He told me that too. The first time was years ago, when I was your age. My mother had brought me here to get a second-hand violin and I was furious, spoilt, because I wanted something new. We were not particularly well off. Not badly off either. Just ordinary.'

I nod.

'The second time he told me,' Ms Black remembers, 'was six, seven years later. The constant cycle of auditions and rejections were grinding me down. I was appalled at the prospect of having to teach others to play while never playing professionally myself. My parents were pressuring me to retrain as a banker or some other utterly sensible thing. I returned to Lev Starman to sell my violin back to him.'

'But you didn't give up?'

'I didn't sell him the violin but I didn't change my mind overnight. I thought about what he'd said. And I realised he wasn't telling me not to play. He meant this: the world is not waiting for anyone to play the violin. Or write a poem. Or paint a picture. Paint, don't paint. Write, don't write. Play, don't play.' She shrugs. 'You may as well play.'

'And then you got a job with an orchestra?'

'Not for a few years. I still struggled. I started up my own chamber group with some other graduates I knew. I began to enjoy teaching. I dabbled with composition. Now, let's stop talking about me. Play something simple. Something you enjoy. What about a G melodic minor? That's my favourite warm-up.'

'Okay.'

I stand for a moment. I let the silence of the weeks I have not played pass through me. *No judgement or fear*, I tell myself. *This is your chance to play.* I draw the bow up, and the music of the scale flows through the room. As the last note lingers, I close my eyes and I play the opening bars of the Mozart.

At first the music flows but then I falter, forgetting the notes. I open my eyes, remembering the other woman in the room. Lev Starman has also returned and is waiting politely in the doorway for me to finish.

'I don't remember the rest,' I say.

'Mozart demands so much of us,' Joanna Black says. 'The notes are not so difficult here, but the expression is unnatural, don't you think? It's hard to understand what he wants us to say.'

'Yes!' I feel a little like crying or like laughing, I'm not sure which. 'Oh, exactly, yes.'

'They say Mozart is too easy for children, and too difficult for artists.'

'Do they?' I ask. 'Do they really say that?'

Lev Starman gives Joanna Black papers to sign. He tells her, 'It will be safe with me. You'll have it back before semester begins. Ms Joanna Black teaches at the Royal Academy of

Music,' he tells me. 'Now, this violin you have just strung, we shall lend this to Ms Black, yes? Until her own violin is finished.'

I have no right to feel disappointed. Why should Starman, or anyone, give me a violin? And yet I feel a sad sharp rift as I hand it over. Once again I am without a violin.

'It was lovely to meet you, Else,' says Joanna Blackman. 'The world might not be waiting for you to play, but I am. Come and see me, please, before you decide to give it up forever.'

Once Joanna goes, I turn to the violin-maker.

'Can I . . . can I help out around here? Cleaning, or, I don't know, filing paperwork or something? To make it up to you.'

'The harm is not permanent,' says Mr Starman. 'But the offer is appreciated.'

I spend the rest of the morning sweeping little curls of wood shavings and dust, emptying the bins.

'You should go now. Adelaide works here on Saturday mornings. She can show you the jobs. You think you can learn to re-hair a bow?'

'Yes! I'd like that. Thank you.'

'There may be another instrument around here you can play in return. Let me see. Oh yes.' He lifts a case from a high shelf. 'It is just a student instrument, nothing special and not of my making. It's just a repair and resell. But for now, on loan to you until you can save up enough to buy a new one.'

'Thank you!'

As I walk through the streets, back to the house on Mortlake Road, I feel the music still, where it is located in the body, my wrist, my fingers, travelling up my arm, vibrating through my sternum and the delicate yet sturdy lines of my rib cage. At the thought of an instrument to play, my step quickens. And then, as if I am still in Australia, as if I am under a huge sky, in the rolling paddocks around the cottage on the hill, I break into a joyful run.

SIBBI

MAMA AND SIBBI step outside Harrods into the light
and each breathes a sigh of relief. Mama looks for the
entrance to the Underground. A big yellow double-
decker bus trundles past covered in writing and colourful
pictures.

Sibbi tugs at Mama's sleeve. Mama has to lean in very
close to hear her.

'What does the writing say?' Sibbi asks.

'Um . . .' Mama reads the side of the bus. 'It says it's
a tourist bus,' Mama says. 'It takes you driving around
all the sights and you can hop on and hop off where
you like.'

'Can we hop on?' Sibbi asks.

'Well,' says Mama. 'Maybe not today.'

'Please?'

'I'm worried about getting lost,' Mama says. 'What if we
hop off and then we can't find our way home?'

Sibbi stares up at her.

Mama sighs. 'You still haven't been to see Baby Prince George yet, have you? Daddy keeps saying he'll take you but he's so busy.'

'Everybody is busy and I am always being so a-lonely.'

'But I *have* been busy, Sibbi, I really do have to finish my thesis.' Mama sighs. 'All right,' she says. 'Where's our sense of adventure? I suppose as long as we can find our way back to the Underground, we can find our way home.'

Mama and Sibbi get on the yellow bus. 'Good grief,' she says when she hears how many English moneys the man wants, but she pays it all and then they go upstairs to find a seat.

'Here we go,' says Mama. 'Here's two just right for us.'

'I want to sit up the front,' says Sibbi.

'But there are already people sitting up the front. We can sit here. We're *nearly* at the front.'

'But I want to be at the front of the front.'

Mama looks up at the older couples sitting in the seats up the front. Both couples are pretending not to hear Sibbi. An older man crosses his arms and sets his mouth in a very hard, straight line.

'We can sit here, Sibbi,' Mama whispers. 'This is the place where we can sit.' Sibbi opens her mouth. 'Or we can get off the bus,' Mama says. And then she says, in a shaky voice that is not like Mama's usual voice, '*Please* don't make a fuss, Sibbi.' The bus begins to rumble away and Sibbi sits down. 'This is fun,' says Mama, but Sibbi thinks it would be more fun if they were at the front of the front of the bus.

Mama studies the little map that came with the tickets. 'Oh look!' she says. 'We're quite close to Buckingham Palace.

And there's Big Ben and Westminster Abbey. Downing Street, and Churchill's war rooms.'

Sibbi doesn't look the map. She looks out the window at green parks and big grand houses. They remind her of the dolls in the store. They have beautiful outsides, but no thoughts. Outhwaite House has its own thoughts.

Mama looks out the window. Sibbi can see Mama but she cannot see Mama's thoughts. She knows they are in there, though.

The bus goes past Trafalgar Square, and Downing Street where the politicians go to work and the Prime Minister lives.

Sibbi thinks Big Ben, the clock tower with the gold face, is the castle where Baby Prince George lives.

Mama shakes her head. 'It's just a clock. Next stop, I think, Sibbi.' And a minute or two later, the driver announces Buckingham Palace. 'Shall we hop off?'

They get off the bus. 'Look,' says Mama. 'The flag's flying. That means she's in.' Mama gives Sibbi a little nudge.

'But I don't think this is the right place,' Sibbi says, frowning.

'Yeah, it is. Look at the guards with their funny hats. See?' Mama points at a very straight-faced guard standing close by.

'But ... but it's all the wrong shape. It doesn't have the pointy bits.'

'Turrets? Mm, I see what you mean. It's not like the castles in storybooks. It does look ... sort of strict and serious, doesn't it? But I think being a queen is strict and serious in real life.'

'Is Baby Prince George strict and serious?'

'I don't think any child can be serious all the time.'

Sibbi walks right up to the fence and presses her face against the railings.

'Shall we go for a walk in the park, or hop on the next bus?' Mama asks.

Sibbi looks at Mama. 'I want to go inside. I want to see the Queen and have tea.'

'Oh honey,' Mama says. 'We're not allowed.'

'But you said she was home!'

'Nobody's allowed to go inside. You know that. You know we can't just walk up to the door.'

Does Sibbi know that? Probably she does, but suddenly it is all too much. She sits down and begins to sob. 'I want to see Baby Prince George, I want to see Ba-ba-ba-by Prince Ge-Ge-George.'

When you are four it can be hard to know what are your parents' rules, and what are the world's rules, and sometimes you blame your parents for things they really have no control over. And when you are a mama, it can be hard to untangle the strands of your child's disappointment, anger and wilful disobedience. And so sometimes you blame your child for things *they* have no control over either.

Sibbi gets angry with Mama. Mama gets angry with Sibbi. Tourists sidestep the two of them as Sibbi flails and beats at Mama and Mama tries to calm Sibbi down. She tries bribing, begging, cajoling, threats of no television.

'What do you *want*?' she asks Sibbi eventually. 'What do you want from me?'

But Sibbi, crying and wailing, does not know what she wants. She just *wants*. She is made of wanting. Wanting is a dark noisy scribble in her eyes and ears and throat and heart.

'Are you going to do something about this child?' a cross man asks as he steps over Sibbi's legs. It is the same man who did not want to give up his front seat on the bus.

'Oh, for goodness sake,' says Mama, galvanised into action by rage (not at Sibbi, at the stern man) and she says a very, very rude word to the man that temporarily stuns Sibbi into silence. She hauls Sibbi, still kicking, into a nearby taxi, and gives the driver the address of Outhwaite House.

About halfway home Sibbi stops howling and quietens to a tired, babyish weeping, and Mama pulls her close and rocks her.

'You feel warm,' says Mama. 'I wonder if you're coming down with something.'

Sibbi rests her head on Mama's shoulder and almost falls asleep, her grubby fingers in her mouth. She is pale and quiet now, tear-stained and dirty from lying on the street.

Mama gives her a little shake to wake her, though she is not really asleep. 'Sibbi, darling, we're home.'

Mama doesn't have enough money in her purse. She gathers Sibbi in her arms, and rings the doorbell of Outhwaite House. Luckily Daddy is home. He comes out and pays the taxi man.

'Do you know how much that cost?' Daddy says to Mama when he comes back into the living room. Mama lays Sibbi down on the couch and smooths her hair, hoping she will fall asleep.

'I honestly don't care,' Mama says. 'I'm just so glad to be back.'

Daddy doesn't say anything more about the taxi money. He says quietly, 'I've just had a call from Australia.'

'And? Was it my parents? Was it my supervisor? Oh, Dave, it's bad news, isn't it?'

'Maybe not in front of Sibbi.'

'I think she's asleep. Sibbi?'

Sibbi keeps her eyes closed.

'It was Bill Wilson on the phone,' Dave murmurs. 'Aunty May's nephew. Aunty May . . . passed away.'

'Aunty May!'

'Not entirely unexpected.'

'But still. It's so sad. She was our friend. She was so kind to us.' Mama sits down next to Sibbi. Sibbi opens her eyes a little. Mama has her hand over her mouth. 'Well, that's it then,' Mama says. 'That's it for the cottage on the hill. We won't be going back now. We won't ever be going back.'

Sibbi closes her eyes again.

'No,' says Dave. 'But we knew that.'

'Did we?' Mama asks softly. 'I suppose we did.'

'He's offered us the chance to buy it – the house and the cottage.'

'Oh, Dave!' Mama's voice rises. 'Really? Could we?'

'Olly! We can't go back. The house, this house . . . it calls on me, in a strange sort of way. I have an obligation. This is our home.'

'The cottage was our home first. It was our home for a long time. Sibbi was born on the lounge-room floor. There's

198

still the stain of it on the floorboards. Oh, Dave. If only we had never inherited this house.'

'But that doesn't make sense either. Before Outhwaite House, before Dorothy, we couldn't have afforded it anyway.'

'We might have been able to,' Mama says, 'if you'd gone back to being a lawyer. How much do they want for it?'

'Market price, maybe even a little less. He's not being greedy. They want to avoid the hassle of putting it on the market. He said if we could agree on a price, we could avoid the real estate fees, and just arrange it through the solicitor. But it's still a lot of money. The market's still booming in Australia.'

'You didn't tell him *no*, did you?'

'I said we'd have to talk about it and he doesn't seem to be in any great hurry. But I said it was unlikely.'

Sibbi listens to the words she knows like *cottage* and *Aunty May* and words she doesn't know like *solicitor*.

She wonders what *passed away* means. She remembers her dream – Aunty May, ready for a journey with her packed suitcase. Perhaps she went away, and then she went *passed* away, until she was very far, very far indeed.

'Why are you home anyway?' Mama asks Daddy.

'Well, I had Jonty recommend somebody to help us with the attic. They're coming this afternoon.'

'What do you mean, like a builder or interior decorator?'

'Well, no. Not really. More like . . . Are you sure Sibbi's asleep?'

'She must be exhausted.'

'Okay, look. I know how this is going to sound. To help us with Sibbi's ghost.'

Mama laughs. 'Oh, wait. *You're serious!*'

'Look, it's getting out of control. This *endsister*. You can't say you don't find it creepy.'

'But you don't actually believe it's a ghost, do you?'

'When I was a kid I thought this house was haunted.'

'Really?'

'I *knew* this house was haunted. I saw ghosts. Two of them. One was, like, an Edwardian nanny or a maid or something. I was never frightened of her. The other was a posh sort of early Victorian teenager. She always looked . . . annoyed. I'd completely forgotten them both until the other night, when we were opening up the attic.'

'Well, I don't know, Dave. A friendly maid and a surly teenager. I mean, even if they *were* real, they don't sound very threatening.'

'But there was always something else too. I was terrified of that door as a kid. Dorothy, my parents, everyone avoided it. It was like they pretended it wasn't there. But whatever was behind the door seemed to work particularly on me. It was like a noise in my head, a persistent buzz, and I'd do things I wouldn't normally do . . . just senseless naughty things, like Sibbi drawing on the wall and cutting Else's violin strings.'

Sibbi is surprised to hear that Daddy heard the buzzing too. She wonders what naughty things little Davey did.

'You think Sibbi is being haunted?' Mama says. 'You think we all are?'

'I knew you'd think that was irrational. But let's say Sibbi believes she is being haunted. Why not ask someone to come and take the ghosts away?'

'It sounds risky. We might just be telling Sibbi that we think the ghosts are real too.'

'The other kids are starting to buy into it. It's getting out of hand. Even I – I can't say I definitely *don't* believe it. What if the ghosts are what's preventing you from really settling in and enjoying London? What if the ghosts are why Else is stealing violins and moping around, and why Sibbi looks so ill all the time?'

'Dave,' says Mama quietly. 'What if we're just unhappy? What if some of us want to be here and some don't? What then?'

'Well, then the worst-case scenario is that this doesn't fix anything. I figure there's no harm in playing along. Play the game out to its logical conclusion.'

'Logical? None of this sounds logical! One minute you're saying ghosts are real, and the next you are saying it's a game.'

'What's the difference between a game and reality?' Dave asks. 'When you live inside a game, it is real.'

Sibbi forgets she is pretending to sleep. She starts to weep. 'I know what an endsister is,' Sibbi says, but, as usual, no one in her family understands the important thing she is trying to say. She *knows* what an endsister is. It's a *kind* of a ghost.

ALMOST ANNIE
AND HARDLY ALICE

'See,' says Almost Annie, nudging Hardly Alice. 'He remembers us.' But as they listen her face drops. 'What does he mean, *take the ghosts away*? Take us where?'

'Dorothy would never have allowed this,' says Alice.

'Well, Dorothy is no longer here,' says Annie. 'Have you ever wondered why that is? Why we are here, but not Dorothy?'

'Dorothy did not pass over at Outhwaite House.'

'Pass over? Oh, you mean die? And yet think of all the people we *have* seen die here. Dorothy's father died in his sleep in the bedroom, and her mother a few months later in the same bed. And there was poor old Mr Arnold who fell down the stairs and Biddy the housemaid, who caught that terrible influenza after the war. And yet here we are. You and I. Why are we ghosts and not any of them?'

'How should I know?' Alice asks. 'Do you think I wanted to spend eternity stuck with you in Outhwaite House?'

'I wasn't even born here,' says Annie. 'I was merely the nurserymaid and my little charges have grown up and so have their children and theirs. It seems at least a little odd that something should hold me to this place. I'd always imagined that in death I'd be restored to the people I loved in life.'

'Humph.'

'Oh, don't be cross. You know I am glad to have you. But despite all these many years, we are still strangers to each other.'

'It is not my fault I have forgotten who I am.'

'And well you may have forgotten, though sometimes I feel certain you must recall something. Tell me this, do you know what was in that attic? I feel it, don't you? Prowling the borders of the house, trapped inside the walls, like a half-starved cat, looking for a way in, or a way out. I hear it whine and then the lights flicker, the screens switch on and off again, plates fall from the shelves. It frightens me, Alice. More than the idea of Dave wanting to get rid of us. More than the thought of the children's poor mother going back to Australia and taking the children with her. It frightens me, but I pity it too. What sort of wounded animal is it? What sort of dark, wild thing?'

'I don't know what you're talking about,' hisses Hardly Alice, haughty with fright. 'There is nothing. There never was anything. It's not here. It's nothing to do with me. Do not speak of it again!'

CLANCY

THE DOORBELL RINGS. I know Dad is busy breaking the unhappy news about Aunty May to Mum, I can hear them talking in the lounge room, though I can't hear what they're saying. It sounds like they're disagreeing about something, but maybe they're just feeling emotional.

I'm hoping it might be Pippa at the door, but a woman is standing on the doorstep. She looks very businesslike, with a clipboard, and a blue suit that kind of shines in the light and high-heeled shoes. She wasn't the sort of person we knew in Australia, but I don't feel terribly surprised to see her here.

'Is your father home?'

'Yes.'

'He's expecting me.'

I leave her on the doorstep. 'Dad!' I go into the lounge room. 'Someone's here.'

Dad jumps up and goes out to the hallway. Mum comes and stands at the lounge-room door, her arms crossed.

'Ms Lane?' Dad says. 'We talked on the phone. Please come in.'

The woman steps into the hallway. 'Please, call me Bridget. You have an occupancy issue?'

'Occupancy?' I ask Mum.

'Ssh,' Mum says. 'I'll explain later.'

'Shall we start with the attic?' Ms Lane asks Dad.

As they ascend the stairs, I turn to Mum again. 'Who is she? What's she doing here?'

Mum shakes her head, looking mostly bewildered. 'She's a spiritual hygienist or something. She's here about Sibbi's ghost.'

'The endsister?'

'Oh, Clancy, really? You don't believe in it too, do you?'

'You have to admit this house is objectively creepy.'

Mum shivers. 'I don't believe in ghosts, Clancy. But I do feel haunted here. By the ornaments and the good china, by the portraits on the wall, the paperwork. It all needs me to make sense of it, and I don't know how.'

'Can I go and watch Ms Lane?' I asked. 'I'm kind of curious. From a scientific perspective.'

Mum nods. 'As long as you stay out of the way.'

'Are you okay?' I say. 'You look tired.'

'I'm always tired, Clancy,' she says, but she never used to be.

I go upstairs.

Dad is saying, 'I can't help thinking that it's my fault. If we could just settle the estate, then the family can settle, and the estate might settle too.'

'Nonsense. Think of it more like a rodent problem. An infestation. Mice don't move into your house because of unresolved history or bad feelings. They move into your house because they are parasites.'

I can't stop myself from saying, 'Mice aren't parasites.'

'Not now, Clancy,' says Dad.

'But mice are mammals, like humans. And they're actually quite intelligent. They form friendships. They bond with their children. You can teach them to answer to their names.'

'Oh, child, don't be foolish. If you don't eliminate mice, they will take over your house. Ghosts are like that too. Look, don't think of them as people. They don't think or feel. They don't want or need anything. They're just bits of leftover energy, disrupting the normal flow of good, clean energy in a house. Sometimes they get tangled up in someone's energy field, usually pets or small children, I find.'

'How do you know ghosts don't think or feel?' I ask. 'Have you ever talked to one?'

'Isn't he clever?' says Bridget Lane, coldly. 'You must be so proud.'

'You said they get tangled up in someone's energy field?' says Dad. 'Could that be what's happening to Sibbi?'

'Almost certainly.' Bridget Lane doesn't sound very worried about Sibbi though. 'Have you thought about selling this house?' she asks. 'I happen to know of an overseas buyer who's interested in converting houses in this area. That's where the real value is. Londoners don't want to maintain houses anymore. Everyone's downsizing into apartments.'

Dad looks confused. 'We're not looking to sell,' he says. 'We just want to get rid of the ghosts.'

Bridget Lane smiles. 'Just thinking out loud. Wait till you've survived a London winter in this big draughty house. You might change your mind about selling. But who knows what the overseas buyers will be investing in by then!'

The front door opens, letting in a quick, noisy blare of light, and the twins tumble inside, arguing about something.

'Goodness,' says Ms Lane. 'Just how many children do you have?'

'Can you help us with the ghosts?' Dad persists. 'This thing about the ghosts getting caught up in Sibbi's energy field has me feeling a bit concerned about Sibbi. She's really not been herself, has she, Clancy?'

And I have to admit, she hasn't.

'Of course. It's a simple procedure. Let me get my equipment from the car.'

Ms Lane passes the twins on the stairs. Finn says hello, but gets no response.

'Who's *she*?' Oscar asks Dad.

'She's here to get rid of Sibbi's ghost.'

'The endsister?' says Finn. 'Is it actually a ghost then? I thought it was only *kind* of a ghost?'

'Oh, wait,' I say. 'I thought she meant a *kind* of ghost like camembert is a *kind* of cheese.'

Finn nods thoughtfully, but Oscar grunts. 'We should have stayed at the park.'

Ms Lane returns with a suitcase. When she opens it up, it's full of electronic equipment, little white plastic boxes that look like phone chargers. 'I'll need to plug one of these in on every floor of the house. Then we'll need to switch them all on at the same time. It disrupts the electrical fields that give ghosts cohesion.'

'Sounds legit,' I say, dryly. I waggle my fingers to make quote marks. '"Science".'

'Will it hurt the ghosts?' Finn asks.

'It will redistribute their energy into the environment,' says Ms Lane.

'But will it *hurt*?' Finn presses. 'Sibbi likes the other ghosts, the teenager ones. She wouldn't want them to be hurt.'

'Teenagers?' Dad asks.

'Don't you listen to *anything* your children tell you?' Oscar asks, and slopes off moodily to his room.

'You stay here, with this one,' Bridget instructs Dad. 'You come with me to the middle floor,' she instructs me. 'And then I'll go down to the ground floor, and when I give the signal, we each turn our boxes on at the same time.'

'Do I have to?' I ask Dad.

'Clancy,' says Dad.

'All right. All right. I don't believe in it anyway.'

Finn waits with me. 'Can't you see the ghosts?' he asks me.

'Of course not,' I say. 'Well, except ... Last night when Dad opened the attic, just for a moment or two, I thought I saw *someone*. I've thought about it and I think it was probably some kind of afterimage. You know when you look at the light globe, and then when you close your eyes, you can still see it? She looked like Else. Well, a bit like Else. I mean it was probably just . . . an after-image of Else. Even though Else wasn't actually in the room at the time.'

'I know who you mean,' says Finn. 'I've seen her. She's moody like Else, and there's something similar about her face, but she's wearing all that old-fashioned gear, nothing like Else wears. And then the other one, she's friendlier, though I think she might be a bit lonely.'

'Do you really *see* them?' I ask. 'Can you see them now?'

'Not all the time. Just glimpses in the background. They don't frighten me though.'

'They don't sound frightening. But whatever was in the attic –'

'It's in the walls now. Listen. It's so high-pitched that it barely registers.'

I listen. 'I can't hear it,' I say. 'But you might just have better hearing than me.'

'Oscar says he can't hear it either.'

'All right,' Bridget Lane calls from downstairs. 'On the count of three.'

'Do you think she has any idea what she's doing?' asks Finn.

'No. I don't think so. Probably not.'

'One, two . . . *three!*'

I flick the switch.

The lights in the stairwell begin to flicker. And suddenly I do hear the high-pitched whine Finn was talking about.

Dad comes down the stairs. 'What do you think, guys? Is it doing anything?'

'Dave,' Mum calls from downstairs. The sound is getting louder, and the lights are going crazy. We go down, Dad, Finn, me, even Oscar. We all crowd into the lounge room. Bridget Lane comes in last.

'This is normal,' Ms Lane says. 'I assure you, this is all perfectly normal.'

Sibbi is sitting up on the couch clutching her ears. 'Stop it,' she whimpers. 'I hate that sound.'

'Is anything happening?' Finn asks Bridget Lane.

'We have to build up enough electricity to scatter the energy,' Ms Lane says.

Whatever is happening, it is happening to Sibbi. She cries, clutching at her ears. 'We hate it,' she says. 'We hate that sound. Stop it. Stop it.'

'I think we've had enough,' Mum says to Bridget Lane. 'Let's switch it off now.'

'This is only the first phase,' says Ms Lane. 'If you turn it off too soon . . .'

Sibbi screams.

'It's hurting her,' Finn says.

'Is it getting rid of the ghosts, though?' asks Dad. He picks Sibbi up and holds her head to his shoulder while she whimpers. 'Is it working?'

'Dave, this is crazy,' Mum says. 'Boys, turn it off.'

'Wait,' Dad tells us.

I look from Mum to Dad to Sibbi.

'What do we do?' Finn asks.

The front door opens with a crash. It's Else. She stands framed by the lounge-room door, crackling with fury.

'*What is going on here?*'

We all turn to Else. Dad looks worried, Mum looks ashamed, Oscar looks interested (he's generally for chaos), and Finn looks frightened. I don't know how I look, but Sibbi looks terrible.

'What is that noise? It's hurting Sibbi? Who are you?' Else demands of Bridget Lane. 'Who's she?' she asks me.

'Turn it off,' says Mum, quiet and firm. 'Turn it off now.'

I run to the middle floor and then upstairs, while Finn flicks the box in the kitchen off. The noise stops, though I think I can still perceive a high-pitched humming in the walls.

We bring back Bridget Lane's devices.

'Fine,' says Bridget Lane, shoving them back into her case. 'Live with them. They'll fill your house with their noise and their mess. They'll suck the energy out of you. They'll give nothing in return. You'll never be truly alone again. They'll be there, all the time, watching, listening, needling. You'll never make them happy.'

'What's she on about?' says Else. 'Is she talking about you kids?'

'Sibbi's ghosts,' Oscar tells Else.

'They're not just Sibbi's ghosts,' says Finn. 'They're everyone's ghosts.'

'I thought you said ghosts didn't want anything,' I say to Ms Lane. 'That they didn't have feelings. That they were just leftover energy.'

'I don't know why people like you insist on living in these gloomy old houses,' says Bridget Lane. 'I grew up in an old house and it never caused my parents or me anything but trouble. I was glad when they finally got divorced, and Mum and I moved out. Give me a brand-new streamlined apartment any day. Bright dazzling white. All new appliances and city views. Not a ghost to be seen. Not a smudge of history in any corner.'

'We don't mind mess, do we, Mum?' says Else. 'We can live with trouble and noise.'

'I'll see myself out,' says Ms Lane.

'We'll all see you out,' says Else, and holds the lounge-room door open.

Ms Lane sniffs, and leaves.

'But did it work?' asks Finn. 'Are the ghosts gone?'

Everybody looks at Sibbi. She sways. 'I know what an endsister is,' she whispers.

'Hush, Sibbi,' says Mum. 'Hush now.' She looks at Dad, and her voice is high and shrill, not like Mum's at all. She sounds haunted. 'I don't like this house, Dave. It's making me sick. It's making Sibbi sick. I know you feel you belong here, and maybe you and the older children do, but I don't. I've been telling myself that I'd never make you choose between me or this house, but I can't stay and I don't think Sibbi can either.'

'What do you mean?' asks Dad. 'Where would you go?'

'I want to go home. I want to go back to Australia.'

ALMOST ANNIE
AND HARDLY ALICE

'I'M STILL HERE,' says Almost Annie, with relief. 'Are you still here?'

There is no reply.

'Alice? Are you still here?'

The house looms emptily around Almost Annie. She has been here dead for much longer than she was ever alive, though time passes quickly to a ghost, or rather time has no meaning and so a ghost will never notice it passing. But there has always been Alice.

'Alice?' Annie calls. 'Are you still here?' She wanders through the hallway where the children are huddled together. *'Did it work?'* Finn is asking. *'Are the ghosts gone?'*

Almost Annie hears these words from very far away. She peers into the kitchen, the formal lounge room, and then drifts up the stairs. The house, full of people, feels lonely, empty.

Annie lingers in the nursery, and in the room that was most recently Dorothy's study but in Annie's lifetime was the governess's quarters. She'd fantasised, in life, of becoming a governess herself, if she could get herself enough education. She listened in on lessons while nursing babies or chasing toddlers and, even while preoccupied with the infants, had picked up Latin faster than any of the Outhwaite children.

As a ghost she'd continued to sit in on the children's lessons, soaking up as much knowledge as she could. She'd watched Dorothy's father grow from a tiny baby to a businessman, learning all about the way a business should be run. In life she'd been restricted, a girl born working class. In death she was able to stroll through all the doors of the house. No knowledge could be kept secret from her. How strange it was to know so much, and yet have such a small existence.

She went up the next flight of stairs into the boys' bedrooms, the parents' bedroom. She thought about what it would be like to be a ghost in the house alone, and began to grieve, for already, even with Alice, it was a lonely existence, a pointless one. What did it matter what she learned, what she knew, if there was no one to share it with?

Finally she went up the steep ladder and into the attic.

And there she was, Hardly Alice, crouched against the wall, hugging her legs, her face shimmering with ghostly tears.

'You're still here!' Annie says. 'Why didn't you answer me? I was calling.'

'I'm still here,' Alice whispers. 'And so are you.'

'Yes,' says Almost Annie. She sits down next to Alice and holds her hand. Though they are both made of insubstantial stuff, there is still a little comfort to be taken from the gesture.

SIBBI

AT FIRST IT is a stain on the wallpaper. Sibbi watches it. The form of it thickens, it's a blob on the wall, and then it's a thing, it's the Endsister. Made of cobwebs and shadows, of dust and forgetting. It creeps across the floor and hunches at the end of the couch where Sibbi lies. No one can see it but Sibbi.

Else sits by Sibbi, stroking wisps of hair out of Sibbi's eyes. 'She's shivering,' Else tells Clancy. 'She's so pale. What were Mum and Dad thinking? What was that woman even doing here?'

Mama comes in. 'The nurse on the National Health Service line says to try giving Sibbi some paracetamol to get her fever down, rather than dragging her out to the medical centre, but we don't have any. Can you keep an eye on her, Else, while I go to the pharmacy?'

'Where's Dad?' Clancy asks.

'He's coming with me. We need to talk.'

'Are you really going back to Australia?' Finn asks. 'What will happen to all of us?'

'Sibbi and I might go back and stay with Nan and Pop for a while.'

Daddy stands unhappily in the doorway. 'Nothing's decided yet,' says Daddy. 'Nobody wants the family to split up.'

Sibbi watches from very far away, from very deep inside her own body. She thinks Mama has decided. Mama won't change her mind now.

When Mama and Daddy have gone, Else looks over at Clancy, who leans forward on the big armchair, watching Sibbi with worry in his face. Finn sits cross-legged on the floor beside the couch.

'What were Mum and Dad thinking?' she asks again.

Finn says, 'They were trying to get rid of the ghosts.'

'But they don't even believe in ghosts.'

'I know what an endsister is,' Sibbi tells Else.

Oscar scowls. 'There's no such thing as ghosts.'

The Endsister – *dust! disappointment!* – stirs.

'Did you hear me?' Oscar says again, loudly. 'There is no. Such. Thing.'

The Endsister swirls and thickens. *Shadows. Dust.* Sibbi cowers.

'Oscar!' says Else.

'What?' says Oscar. 'If you really want to know, I'm sick to death of all of you. I'm sick of this family. It's all about Else and her violin. Or Sibbi and her precious endsister. Or Clancy and Pippa. No one's ever asked me what I think about moving to England. No one ever thinks about what I want. It's just Oscarandfinn. Finnandoscar. Nobody cares about me.'

Rage. Rage. Sisters and sisters. Brothers and brothers. Sharp tongues. Quarrelling squabbles, squabbling quarrels. This is what the Endsister wants. This is what it grows fat on.

'I know,' moans Sibbi, 'I know what an endsister is.'

'You're such a baby,' says Oscar. 'It's not an *endsister*, you idiot. It's an *ancestor*.'

'What did you say?' says Else. 'Endsister,' she says experimentally. '*Ancestor*.'

No! The Endsister pushes upwards now, she's a real thing, coming into being – endsister, endsister. That is the name of her. Sister. Endsister.

Oscar keeps on at Sibbi. 'It's an *ancestor*,' he says again. 'Not a ghost. It's, like, your grandmother's grandmother. Your aunty's aunty's aunt.'

No! No! Rage. Rage. Endsister is rage. Abandoned. Wasps and spider husks. Endsister is revenge. Swirling. Swirling. Tit for tat, measure for measure, eye and tooth, eye and tooth. Endsister.

'Can you smell that?' Clancy asks.

'Can anyone see that thing?' says Finn, rubbing his shining, watery eyes, though they only seemed to become waterier and waterier.

'What's that noise?' asks Else. 'What's that awful noise?'

THE BLACK CLOUD grows darker and bigger, pulling into itself all the dust, all the dark. Now all the children can feel its presence. The cloud feeds on their fear and sorrow and envy and rage.

Sibbi feeds it. All her fears of being abandoned or unloved or not listened to, of being left behind, a baby forever, as the other children grow and grow. Other fears too, the regular fears of childhood: fears of the dark, and giants, wolves, of things that swoop or crawl or wait in the hidden corners of night.

It feeds from Else, all her whirling self-hatred and shame, the waste of money and time and happiness, the loss of her violin. The cage of unhappiness she built around herself. *No!* Else tries to tell herself. *Things are getting better.* But suddenly it seems to Else that happiness is fleeting, and it can never last.

Clancy feeds it too. He thinks of the girls on the bus back in Melbourne, teasing him all the way home. He imagines that Pippa is there too, that she sits next to him on the bus and the girls start up with their teasing and he can't defend himself or Pippa. What would she think of him if she saw who he really was?

And how long has Oscar secretly hated being a twin? Oh, the Endsister stirs it all up, that secret longing in Oscar to be out in the world on his own, without Finn always there, a mirror showing Oscar who he is and who he is not, limiting who he might be, given a whole chance. A twin never gets a *whole* chance. All a twin can ever expect is half. Half a chance. Half a life.

Finn feels it all, spinning through the room. It's like his family's feelings all pass through him, the loneliness, the anxiety, the despair, the jealousy, the self-loathing. Finn feels all of it, as if the family itself is spinning up there, in that bitter black cloud, spinning apart into pieces, no longer a whole, wonderful, messy thing, but parts of something broken. He can hardly bear it.

Dave and Olly walk down the street towards the pharmacy, and they feel it too, filled with the hopelessness of their situation. Olly can't stay and Dave can't leave. *Is this how a marriage ends?* Olly wonders. *I still love Dave, but I can't live this life.*

Is this how a marriage ends? Dave wonders. *Can you love someone and let them go at the same time?*

The Endsister eats the darkness that leaks from the split between them.

'It's too loud,' says Sibbi. 'It's so loud. It's all the noise inside me.'

'But,' says Else, realising. '*I* know this noise. It's from inside me too.' She looks around the room. 'And from Finn, and Oscar, and Clancy.' And then she has a flash of understanding. 'I think I know what to do,' says Else.

ELSE

THE LOUNGE-ROOM DOOR slams behind me, and the hallway is quiet and still. The violin case is just inside the front door, where I left it. I open the case, take out the violin, and place it on my shoulder, and plucks the strings, listening. I feel the strings inside myself, my own longing and desire, certainty and doubt, being plucked. *Plink plink plink.* I pull out the bow and dance it across the strings. The sound is good enough – thin, a little constricted, it *is* only a student violin – but it will do.

I hold the instrument and its bow in one hand and push at the living room door but it's stuck. I shout for the boys, thump at the door, but I can't get it to open, and, trapped in that room, with all that energy whirling around, they don't seem to be able to hear me.

ALMOST ANNIE
AND HARDLY ALICE

Almost Annie and Hardly Alice watch from the stairs. 'We need to help her,' says Almost Annie. 'Please. We need to help the children.'

Alice passes her hand over her eyes.

Annie says, 'You know, don't you? You've been here longer than me. You know what was in the attic. You must know.'

'But I *don't* know,' cries Alice. 'I don't *know* what I know.'

Else pushes at the door, but the force of the wind – the Endsister – pushes back. Annie and Alice push too, one on either side of Else. Almost Annie, Hardly Alice and Else use all their anger, their rage and disappointment, the things they've lost, the things they've left behind, the most tattered parts of themselves. They push on the door, three teenage girls, each of a different time, but all the same pattern of longing and loss, the warp and weft of presence and absence.

The door gives way and Else staggers inside.

ELSE

'YOU'VE GOT A violin,' says Clancy as I burst into the living room at last. 'How can you have a violin?'

I don't explain. I close my eyes, and start to play the Mozart. Easy for a child, difficult for an artist. And it's so, so hard. My hands, are soft with lack of practice. The strings cut into my fingers. But I play on.

At first all I can hear are mistakes, dead music being forced out of a lifeless instrument. My mistakes feed the cloud, the dark whorl of disappointment, despair, loss, sorrow, abandonment, pain ... it gobbles up my mistakes and grows fatter.

I realise I'm holding my breath. My shoulders are tense and my arms are stiff. I stop playing for a moment, put the violin under my arm in rest position and roll my shoulders backwards and forwards. I stretch my neck from one side to the other. I breathe: in, out ... in, out ... in ... out. I feel my chest expand and contract. I place my feet squarely on the floor. I draw my attention up my spine, aware of each knobbly vertebra, and down to the tips of my fingers. *No one is asking you to play the violin. Play, don't play.* I raise my instrument again.

I picture Sibbi, back home in Australia, running, playing, imagining, climbing, hiding, seeking, rolling down the hills, resilient as a grass flower, the wind rushing through the reeds, white clouds racing across the sky. I see myself too – the child I once was – spinning in my orbit between Olly and Dave, fierce and determined.

You may as well play.

The bow hovers over the string, and the music begins. I am not playing the Mozart. The music is playing me, giving itself form and spirit inside my body. The cloud takes form too, at first a funnel of dark smoke, and then something with a shape, with a form, with a spirit of its own.

ALMOST ANNIE
AND HARDLY ALICE

'WHAT IS IT?' asks Annie, curious rather than frightened, as the form finds its shape. And then, '*Who?*'

'Who?' echoes Hardly Alice. 'Oh, who . . .?' She squeezes her eyes shut, not to hide this time, not to deny, but to remember.

'Think, Alice. What *don't* you know?'

'I don't know who I am.'

'What else don't you know? You were alive once, alive in this house. You like the boys – you had brothers? You had a father. A mother.'

'My mother? *She* took my mother from me.'

'The ghost? The Endsister took your mother?'

'The Endsister? Yes, yes. My mother had a baby, and the baby lived, but my mother died. The baby. My sister.' Hardly Alice looks at Almost Annie. 'I remember. I remember everything.'

'What do you remember?'

Alice whirled, and pointed at the black cloud. 'Beatrix!'

The music plays on, but the air grows still, poised, listening.

'Beatrix Elizabeth Rose Outhwaite, you behave yourself this instant. I am your sister and you will do as you are told.'

The shape thickens and slows, comes together, spinning more slowly now. *Beatrix? Elizabeth? Rose? Outhwaite?*

Forgotten. Lost. Beatrix? Elizabeth? Rose?

Almost forgotten. Not yet lost.

Annie gasps. Hardly Alice stands tall. The music hovers, an extended moment of time – a *ghost* moment of *ghost* time. All the Outhwaite children remain inside the stillness and the silence between notes, but the littlest ghost girl wriggles herself into being. *Sorry, not sorry. Sorry, not sorry.*

SIBBI

LATER NONE OF the Outhwaites would quite agree what happened.

'She was a girl,' says Sibbi. 'The Endsister.'

'*Ancestor*,' Oscar will correct.

'Ancestor,' Else agrees, absently. But: 'Of course there's no such thing as ghosts. Is there?'

'Of course not,' Clancy will say. 'There is definitely no such thing as ghosts. Definitely.'

'There was a girl who didn't know she was a girl,' says Sibbi. 'She thought she was dust. Except she wanted to play with me.'

'There was no girl,' says Oscar.

'There was something with the electrics, I think,' says Finn, doubtfully. 'It got dark.'

'Beatrix,' says Sibbi. 'Her name was Beatrix. Else played her back. She was lost, but Else found her.'

'I was lost,' Else says. 'But then I understood what I needed to do.'

'Of course there's no such thing as ghosts, Sibbi,' says Mama. 'You have such a big imagination.'

'But there really was a Beatrix,' Daddy will tell them. 'That's a coincidence, isn't it? In Aunt Dorothy's family tree.' He brings the hand-drawn family tree down from the study. 'Look. She's the younger sister of my great-great-great grandfather. And she died when she was two. One of the Victorian diseases, I suppose – cholera or diphtheria. Their older sister, Alice, died the same year.'

'Oh, how sad, look,' says Mama, pointing. 'Their mother must have died giving birth to Beatrix, the date of her death is the same as Beatrix's birthday.'

'I told you,' says Oscar. 'I told you. Not *endsister*. Ancestor.'

'Okay. You were right. You don't have to be smug,' says Else.

But it isn't often Oscar gets to be the clever one. He can't help enjoying it. 'Can I sleep in the attic then?' he asks Mama and Daddy. 'If Sibbi is going to move back in with Else?'

'The attic creeps me out,' says Finn.

'There's no such thing as ghosts,' Clancy says again. 'Definitely. Definitely. No such thing.'

'You sure about that?' says Else.

'Of course,' says Clancy. 'Aren't you?'

'They're gone anyway,' says Sibbi. 'All of the girls. Gone now.'

'Gone where?' Finn asks, curiously.

'Away. Away and then *past* away.'

'That's that then,' says Daddy. 'No more ghosts. See? I told you it would work.'

BEATRIX ELIZABETH ROSE

'BEATRIX ELIZABETH ROSE Outhwaite, behave yourself this instant. I am your sister and you will *do as you are told*.'

Beatrix Elizabeth Rose Outhwaite – for once in her life and in her long, long, lonely death – does as she is told.

She stands in the middle of the room, blinking. For the ghosts, it is the living who now become insubstantial. The Outhwaite children – Else, Sibbi, Clancy, Oscar, Finn – fade to almost nothing at the edges of the room.

'At last!' breathes Annie. 'A babe I can hold.'

She scoops Beatrix Elizabeth Rose into her arms. Beatrix lays her head on Annie's shoulder, sticks her fingers in her mouth – same two fingers as Sibbi – and peeps out shyly at Alice.

'Your *sister*?' says Annie. 'Your sister.'

'My sister,' confesses Alice. 'I had forgotten her. I had forgotten everything. And then Else brought the remembering. It came on the music, like a river sweeping through me. I almost remembered before, so many times, but I didn't want to. I wanted to forget, so I forgot.'

'But why? Why would you want to forget her?'

'I will tell you, but you might hate me. She was born, and my mother died. Perhaps she missed Mother too, for in her first year, she screamed more than not. Nobody wanted her. Not my father, who was heartbroken, nor my brothers, James and Sebastian. My father, unable to cope with us all, sent the boys to boarding school, so I lost not only a mother but also my brothers, and in return was left with a change-ling, or that was how I felt about her. Father left me to hire the nurses, and I chose only those with kind faces and caring hearts, so that they could love her as we could not. My own heart was closed to her, I willed it so.'

'You were a child,' says Annie. 'You had lost your mother.'

'I was bitter. I blamed *her*.'

'You were a child,' says Annie again, with love. 'A grieving child.'

'When she got sick, Father believed it was her violent emotions that caused her fever and had her confined to the attic. I asked the nurse to make it comfortable for her, and I thought to check on her by and by, but I had grown ill myself. She upstairs and I in this very room must have died our separate lonely deaths, for when I woke from death, it was to discover my father locking up the attic in his grief and guilt. He left the house after that and for many years the house was empty. Everything left me. My family, my history, my memories, until all that was left was my name, and hardly even that. When the family returned, I did not recognise them or myself.'

'And Beatrix?'

'In the attic all that time. Too young to even have her name, or to know what she was, to hold on to the shape of herself. I at least had that.'

'And you knew she was there?'

'I knew *something* was in there. I was afraid of it, and I pitied it. The way one might feel about a wild, wounded animal. I also knew it belonged to me, and that I didn't want it. I didn't want to own its wildness, its wounds, or my own wounds for that matter. So I forgot. And she protected herself, keeping people away from the attic by the sheer obstinate force of her will.'

Annie smiles. 'Her will. Your will. How alike you are. And now you remember everything?'

'And *she* remembers,' Alice says. 'Most importantly, she remembers being Beatrix. Beatrix Elizabeth Rose Outhwaite. She is here and I am here.'

'And me,' Annie says. 'I am here too. I wonder why?'

Hardly Alice does not have the answer. 'In death I had little interest in the living. They came and went, driven by clocks and calendars, while time congealed around me, a frying egg white thickening around its yolk. I paid none of you any attention, but one day you were there, the same as me. Dead, like me, and yet living on, in phantom form. Extraordinary. And yet ordinary, with your plain way of speaking and your bonny face, like sunshine entering a room, making the dust twinkle.'

Almost Annie kisses Beatrix Elizabeth Rose Outhwaite's forehead. 'Poor wee babe,' she says. 'You tragic children.' And she passes Beatrix over to Alice.

'Me?' says Alice, fumbling as she takes Beatrix in her arms. 'I've never held a baby before. Well perhaps my brothers, when I was young.'

'And now your sister,' says Annie.

Beatrix tolerates Alice for a moment. She reaches up to touch her face, then pull her hair, then wriggles to be put down. She takes Annie's hand and tugs on it.

'I've always had a way with children,' Annie says, apologetically. 'Or they've had a way with me.'

'Yes,' says Alice. 'There's your answer. She wanted you. She wanted a nursemaid more than a sister. What's a sister to her?'

'Well,' says Annie, 'she has us both now. And we have each other, Alice. You and I.' *You were a child too*, thinks Annie, *a haunted, wounded child. And it was your job to pick the maids. Perhaps you chose me.*

'Where on earth is she going?' Alice asks.

The little ghost Beatrix leads the big ghostly girls down to the front door, which is open, letting in the sweet air of the summer afternoon. A bicycle goes past, and children at play call to each other, and a dog barks somewhere.

'We can't go out there,' Annie says to Beatrix. 'It's not for us, that world.'

'No,' says Alice, thoughtfully. 'We can't go *out there*. But I have a feeling – do you? – I have a feeling we *can* go through that door.'

'I'm not frightened,' says Annie. 'Are you?'

'Of course not,' says Alice, and she takes Annie's free hand in hers. This way the three ghosts proceed, going first away and then passed away, into the place where only the dead may go, and never, ever the living.

ELSE

'ARE YOU REALLY going to take Sibbi back to Australia?'
I ask Olly, as we sit side by side, wrapping teacups in paper and
gently nestling them in boxes, ready for auction. Since Sibbi's
Endsister has gone, the house feels lighter, fresher. Dave has
stopped going to Mr Brompton's office every day. He's trying
to clean out Aunt Dorothy's study, while Olly is takes a break
from writing her thesis to tackle the kitchenware.

'It's the strangest thing,' Olly says. 'Dad and I fought
all the way to the chemist. He was insisting we had to stay,
and I knew I needed to leave, and take Sibbi with me, that
she would never thrive here. Honestly, Else, my heart was
breaking. I was sure our marriage was ending. I was gutted.'

'Mum!'

'And then we bought the medicine and we were walking
home, and it was like something, *something* just lifted.
I could hear you playing in the house, and the sun was rich
and golden. The sky was grey, isn't the sky always grey here?
But it was a marvellous, luminous grey, the light seemed to

bounce off it. And then we did a total switch. Dave suddenly felt that he could leave, and I suddenly felt that I could stay.'

'So we're staying?' I asked.

'I don't know. We still don't know if we can afford to keep Outhwaite House. Bridget Lane gave Dave the idea of turning it into two big apartments, and we could keep one and sell the other. Jonty is an architect, of course, so he could help us.'

'Oh, it seems a shame to carve up Outhwaite House.'

'Yes, I agree. And I am not sure I'm keen on raising Sibbi in an apartment. The cottage was small, but . . .'

'At least Sibbi had trees to climb.'

'Did you know that Aunty May's nephew offered to sell us the cottage and Aunty May's house?'

I have a sudden image of the cottage on the hill, the galahs swooping over, and a massive wave of longing almost overwhelms me.

'But you seem happier here, now,' Olly says. 'Aren't you? You have your violin, and your Star Man and a contact at the Royal Academy. And could we really take Clancy away from Pippa? The twins seem to have settled in fine and Sibbi's finally let her imaginary Endsister go.'

'Hm,' I say. 'Hm.'

'You think we should go back to Australia?'

'I think you should ask us.'

'Put it to the vote, you mean?'

'I just think you should at least ask.'

So that night, Olly makes two lasagnes, a veggie one and a meat one, and we sit in the kitchen, together.

Dave tells Clancy and the twins and Sibbi about Aunty May's house and the nephew's offer.

'We'd have to sell Outhwaite House,' Dave says. 'But we might have to anyway. It's a big expensive house, and we have to pay the government a lot of tax for inheriting it. And even if we can afford that, there's rates and heating bills and maintenance – it's an old house and it needs work.'

'Dad are you heartbroken? I thought you loved this house,' says Clancy.

'I felt beholden to it,' Dave says. 'I felt I owed it something, or that I owed Dorothy something. But when I thought I might have to choose between Outhwaite House and Olly . . . well. It's just a house.'

'We *could* sell Outhwaite House and buy somewhere else in London,' says Olly. 'Somewhere that doesn't need so much work. We could even move to the English countryside. Pippa could come and visit on weekends, or you could come down to London, Clancy. And Else, maybe you could keep your job with the violin-maker. We could find a way for that.'

'Or we could move back to Australia?' says Oscar.

'We all move back or we all stay?' asks Finn. 'Whatever we decide, we all do it together?'

'Yes,' says Olly.

'Together,' says Dave.

'Then I don't care,' says Finn. 'As long as we're together.'

'What about you, Else?' says Olly.

'I can play violin anywhere,' I say. 'It's not really up to me. In a few years I'll be old enough to move out. Then I can live wherever I want. But in the meantime, if I had to choose, then I'd say Australia.'

'Me too,' says Finn. 'If I had to choose.'

Olly turns to Clancy. 'What do you think Clancy? Could you bear to leave Pippa?'

I watch the pain drift across his face. But: 'I'd choose Australia too,' says Clancy. 'If it was up to me.'

'Really?' I say.

'I don't know why you're all so surprised,' Clancy says gruffly. 'I mean, I'll miss Pippa. Of course I will. And if you all wanted to stay here, I'd adapt. That's what living things do. They grow and develop and respond to their environment, and I can do all those things. But Australia is my habitat. Anyway, Pippa and Jonty are already planning to take a trip to Australia, so it's not like I'll never see them again.'

'Would we live in the cottage or Aunty May's house?' says Sibbi.

'Good question!' Olly says.

'We could live in one while we fix up the other, and then swap around,' says Dave. 'We'll get a lot more money for Outhwaite House than it will cost us to buy Aunty May's place. We'd have money to renovate, and a bit of money to put away for each of you kids. Else, you really would be able to study anywhere in the world.'

'Oscar, are you crying?' Olly says.

Oscar wipes tears away from with the back of his hand. 'Yes,' he says. 'But I'm not sad. I just really, really want to go home.'

SIBBI

HERE COMES SIBBI Outhwaite, skipping down the kangaroo track. Still wild, still made of sunshine and shadows, but her face is narrowing, and sharpening, she's losing some of the softness of the jaw. She's five now.

Butterflies flutter in the grass. It's December. Flocks of cockatoos settle to strip the seeds from the wallaby-grass.

A wedge-tail eagle soars overhead, hunting food for his twin hatchlings. Aunty May told Sibbi the story of Bunjil the creator spirit, who, in the time before time, made this valley and all the land. Bunjil took the form of an eagle, so he could look down from the sky and keep an eye on things. Stories live and breathe. This one breathes inside Sibbi.

'Wedge-tailed eagles mate for life,' Clancy tells Sibbi, coming up behind her on the track. 'The mummy and daddy eagles build the nest together, and take turns looking after their babies. Wedge-tailed eagles live in a huge terri-tory' – Clancy spreads his arms wide, *huge* – 'and have lots of nests, but they usually have a favourite one, which they use over and over. I finally found his nest today. It's probably really old.'

'Show me.'

Clancy shakes his head. 'It's bedtime. Come on, the bats will be out soon. There's the first star.'

'It's for wishing on,' says Sibbi and she stops in the path, but she can't think of even one wish. From the house comes the sound of Else's violin, notes climbing upwards to Bunjil's sky.

'Come on,' says Clancy. 'You're blocking the path. Anyway, I don't believe in wishes.'

'I was wishing I could see the eagle nest,' says Sibbi.

'Tomorrow,' says Clancy. 'I'm going to take some photos of it to send to Pippa.'

'See,' says Sibbi. 'Wishing is true.'

ELSE

OLLY STANDS AT the window, looking up at the cottage on the hill, just as she once stood at the window of the cottage on the hill, looking down at this house on the road. I pack up my violin but the song of it lingers in the air, the melodies resonate inside me, long after I finish playing.

'Remember Sibbi's ghosts?' Olly asks Dave.

'I wonder if *she'll* remember them?' I say. 'I wonder if she'll remember London at all?'

'She'll remember the story of London,' says Olly. 'We'll tell the story of London forever. Our big journey. Our lucky story.'

'Oh, stories,' says Dave. 'Slippery things, those stories. Hard to catch them in your hand.'

I look at my own outstretched hand, as if I might catch one. And I do – I remember, with sudden vividness, the bird in the cage, Sibbi's bird, in Hong Kong, a song in a bird in a cage in a city. How lost I had been. *Poor, silly, lost Else,* I think now, with fondness and pity and curiosity and joy.

CLANCY

D<small>USK</small> <small>FALLS</small>, <small>A</small> gentle, forgiving, powdery dark. Oscar and Finn call to each other across the house. Sibbi looks upwards, believing in the stars. I take a mental photograph to send Pippa.

I tell her a story in my mind, all the way across the world.

I tell her a story like this one, a story that spreads its wings, that is guided by stars, a story that is a flightpath and also a song, singing itself into being. A story that ends where it begins: a story about coming home.

I KNOW WHAT AN ENDSISTER IS

It was my middle child, Una, aged five at the time, who first conjured the Endsister, and her older sister, Frederique, who a few days later corrected her, giving this story its beginning and its end. One night, around the same time, I had a dream that my best friend gave birth to a baby girl and called her Annie Hardly Alice. It was Fred who had her heart broken in the bird markets in Hong Kong when she was five years old, and Kirsty Murray who pointed out what a fascinatingly male-centric space the bird market is. It was me who wrote a couple of years later, in the midst of a devastating period of writer's block,

The world is not waiting
for you to write a poem
Write. Don't write.
You may as well write.

I don't know how all these things (and countless other small moments) coalesced in my brain to make a story, but I know why they did, and that is because in 2014 I received an email from Molly O'Neill, who was working with Storybird.com, asking me if I would consider pitching a serialised novel for their creative partnership programme. So *The Endsister* began its life online, published chapter by chapter over the course of a year, on Storybird. It was read and liked and commented on by people of all ages all over the world. It feels strange to think now that what was basically a first draft of *The Endsister* still exists out there on the internet. Writers usually like to hide their work, but it's out there, in its rawest form for anyone to read. I wonder if you could learn something – about writing, about me – by making a comparison between the two?

During the time I was writing and publishing *The Endsister* on Storybird, my father, Bob Russon, died. The community of readers on Storybird kept me motivated to write during this time, their love of Sibbi and her family kept her real in a time when making up stories may have felt like a fool's errand. My dad would have liked Sibbi; a primary school teacher, he had an enduring love and respect for children and childhood – something we shared. He was born in England like Dave, but halfway through his life came to Australia as a ten-pound Pom, met my mum, Frances, and together they made a home and a family in Tasmania.

Huge thanks to Molly O'Neill, Mark Ury and everyone at Storybird, especially all the other Creative Partners and young people in the Storybird community who read, liked, shared and commented. I'd particularly like to thank Victoria Usova who drew Sibbi, the twins, Else, Clancy, Dave and Olly and the ghost girls for Storybird, and made them come alive for me, even before the writing began. Thanks to Sandra Eterović and Sandra Nobes for the cover of my dreams, and to Eva Mills and Hilary Reynolds for helping me reimagine a serialised story into a solid book – a bit like trying to catch a river in your hands. Thanks also to Penny Harrison, Chay Baker, Chris Miles, Lili Wilkinson, Sarah Dollard and Kate Whitfield, who either helped me solve plot problems or just asked interested questions. Thanks to Ange, Daniel, Ashleigh and all the crew at Wild Wombat, where I am writing these words. Thanks to all my Blogger, Twitter, Facebook, Instagram and IRL friends for being funny and interesting and outraged and compassionate. Thanks to my family for putting up with me.

Thanks to me, for writing this book. The world might not have been waiting, but I was.

And thank you, for reading.

ABOUT THE AUTHOR

Penni Russon grew up in Tasmania and now lives in a house built by a drama teacher in the foothills of the Kinglake Ranges – Wurundjeri country. She lives with her partner, three kids and a schnauzer called Swoosie.